Discovery

A Collection

by Ginger Simpson

ISBN-13: 978-1496167866

ISBN-10: 1496167864

Electronic edition of *Discovery* published by:

Books We Love Ltd.

Chestermere, Alberta

Canada

ASIN: B00IP06KFG

Copyright 2014 Ginger Simpson

Cover art copyright 2014 by Michelle Lee

:

Contents

A Wing and a Prayer

Callie Corwin passed down the aisle of the 757 one more time before takeoff. Her heart thudded in her chest like the jet engines. Hopefully, she'd done everything by the book. This was her first flight as an attendant, and everything she'd learned during training seemed to have gotten lost in her muddled thoughts of the training manual and its long checklist of things to do.

Making her way back to her own seat in the front of the plane, she halted at a huge pair of cowboy boots blocking the aisle. "Excuse me, sir." She jostled the muscular shoulder of a person in repose, most of his face hidden by a black Stetson.

He lifted the hat higher on his head and pulled his long, lanky legs back into place. "Yes?"

She swallowed hard, seeing eyes bluer than a Montana sky staring back at her. "Y…you'll have to buckle your seatbelt for takeoff." Her gaze drifted down the length of him and rested on his bag. "And you'll have to stow your carry-on under the seat in front of you."

"Yes, ma'am." He doffed the brim of his hat and nudged the black case forward with his foot.

She tried to be professional and not chuckle at his adorable accent. With a smile and a fluttery stomach, she turned and continued to her jump seat in the galley. That cowboy certainly was a piece of eye candy. Too bad there wasn't time to get better acquainted. Still, the eleven-hour flight from California to England would certainly offer another chance.

She harnessed herself in and smoothed her hands across her skirt. So far, so good. No one had gotten angry, everyone found their allotted seat, and the safety instructions had gone off without a hitch. Of course, no one really followed along with the pamphlet in the seatbacks, but at least she managed her safety belt demonstration without dropping her prop. She never expected to be so nervous. Her palms dampened even now as her fellow flight attendant announced they'd been cleared for takeoff.

Flying backward always bothered her. Why couldn't they have put the crew's seats on the opposite wall? As the airplane picked up speed, she closed her eyes and took a deep breath, planting both feet firmly on the floor. On the climb, turbulence swayed the fuselage, and Callie's fingers clenched into a knot in her lap. "Bumps in the road," she muttered, reminding herself of the words her instructor had shared. She'd flown many times in her twenty-two years, but she'd never get used to the roughness caused by air currents. As she often did as a passenger, she counted backwards from one hundred. Usually before she got to twenty-five, things smoothed out. This time was no different.

After a cleansing breath, she opened her eyes and then fidgeted to find her gaze locked with those Montana blues again. Just her luck. The aisle seat of row four had a perfect view of her seating area and at this moment, *her*. She managed a weak smile and prayed for the captain's signal to begin in-flight service. Diverting her attention, she turned to chat with the attendant sitting next to her but warmed from the heat of seat 4C's blazing stare.

As soon as the plane leveled and the buzzer sounded, Callie flexed both fists on the armrests, took a deep breath, and unfastened her safety belt. Pasting on a smile, she rose, and forcing herself, she took calm, measured steps across the aisle and back to the galley.

Behind the privacy divider, she pulled sodas from the icebox and prepared them for the orders her fellow crewmember was already taking in the plane's forward section. The aft handled their own. She lined the cans by type and mentally ran through her list of duties. Once the drinks and light refreshments were served, she'd pass through the cabin, offering pillows and blankets. Maybe she'd heat a bottle for a baby, or help an elderly person to the bathroom. Whatever was needed for the passenger's comfort, she'd do.

Unbidden, the image of that angular jaw and those piercing blue eyes filled her head, and she cut herself on a pop-top. She pressed her finger against her lips, winced, and then grimaced at the salty taste of blood. After dipping a napkin into melted ice, she dabbed at the painful slice and then removed the first aid kit from the shelf below the counter, found a band-aid, and applied the skin-colored strip to her wound. Even behind the panel separating her from the passengers, she scrunched her face into a worrisome wince, knowing the handsome cowboy waited to ogle her again. Darn, why couldn't seat 4C have been 28B instead of the constant distraction he'd become?

The plane lurched upward. Callie grabbed the counter and narrowed her widened eyes. Would she ever get used to those dratted bumps? A buzzer summoned her. She checked the lights above the seats for the passenger who rang—9D. As she made her way down the aisle, Mr. Eye Candy lowered the lashes of one eye in a definite wink. Pretending to ignore him, she continued past, fighting against showing her obvious attraction. Drat! The guy really tested her resolve, and she couldn't afford to be sidetracked when she was trying to prove herself on the job. Besides, fraternizing with passengers must be listed somewhere on the forbidden activity list.

A dark-complexioned man sat beneath the lit service light. Callie released his call button. "May I help you, sir?"

He thrust his plastic glass at her. "I want more." He spoke with a heavy accent, unfamiliar to her. Beneath bushy brows, his dark eyes and thin lips conveyed an aura of ice.

"Of course. I'll be happy to refill your glass. What were you drinking?" The spicy aroma of his aftershave hinted at Whiskey. She hoped he had the correct change as she had none.

"Tonic with a twist of lime."

She figured him for something much stronger but nodded. "I'll be right back."

As she turned, he removed a cell phone from his pocket, flipped open the top and started to dial.

"I'm sorry, sir." She reached toward his hand. "You aren't allowed to make calls during flight, unless you use the phone in the seatback in front of you."

The man stared at her with ebony contempt, recoiling from her intended touch as if she might infect him with something. "Do not dare touch me."

Callie straightened and pressed her hand to her throat. "I'm sorry, sir. I meant no disrespect. I simply—"

"Is there a problem here?" someone asked.

Callie turned, leveling her eyes on a familiar checkered shirt pattern. She raised her gaze to the handsome face of the man from seat 4C. "N…no. There's no problem."

The two passengers exchanged glares before the

cowboy brushed past. "I need to use the john in the back. Someone must be taking a nap in the front one."

Callie swallowed her chuckle, cleared her throat, and turned back to the seated passenger. "I'm sorry if I offended you, sir. I'll be right back with your drink."

In the galley, her cheeks flamed as she wrestled with her thoughts. On one hand, the protective attitude of the man in seat 4C flattered her but insulted her on the other. She'd gone through courses on how to deal with difficult personalities, but her training didn't cover what to do when a handsome cowboy rode in to your rescue. She detested dealing with the rude man again, but sighing, refilled his glass with ice and tonic water. Fixing a friendly smile on her face, she squared her shoulders and made her way down the narrow aisle. The flight had barely begun and already she wondered if she'd made the right career choice.

* * * *

Callie held the basket out in front of her. "Would you like some peanuts?" She couldn't very well pass up *his* row, although the masculinity he exuded made her stomach do flip-flops.

The other two passengers seated to his left took packets and tore into the foil as if they hadn't eaten in months. The handsome cowboy balanced his hat on his knee, leaned back in his seat with arms behind his neck and shook his head. "No, ma'am, wouldn't care for any, thank you." His gaze wandered over her from head to toe.

"Can I put your hat in one of the overhead bins?" She fidgeted, feeling naked to his stare, and then grasped the latch above her head.

"No thanks. I'll keep it. I plan to take a nap, and my Stetson blocks out the light."

His shock of sandy hair, flattened by his hat, begged to be fluffed. She showed great restraint and denied the urge. The rumpled look did nothing to hamper his appearance. She moved along, serving peanuts to the rest of her area and then returned to the galley and stowed the remaining packets. Something niggled at her about the dark man with the foreign accent, but she forgot about her worries when Margo, her friend and recent flight school graduate, elbowed her. "Did you get a load of that hunk in aisle four? The passenger manifest says his name is Troy Willows."

"Troy, eh?" Callie nibbled her lip. "Hmm, I was thinking something more along the lines of Rock... or Spencer. He doesn't strike me as a Troy...and Willows? More like a mighty oak, if you ask me. Did you check out those thighs?"

Margo chuckled. "How about those guns? The man definitely works out."

Callie glanced over her shoulder and then turned back with a sly grin. "He can work out with me anytime." Her cheeks warmed at her own admission, and she looked for a reason to move on to something else. She smoothed her hair back behind her ears and checked her watch. "It's time to start the movie."

"What are we playing today?" Margo opened the door housing the video components and plopped in a disc. She held up the DVD case and laughed. "It's the latest James Bond movie. How appropriate."

The murmuring of voices quieted as the show began. Callie pulled out a clipboard and turned on a muted light above the galley counter. "We might as well check the special food requests against the seating chart. When Mr. Bond has killed all the villains, everyone will be ready to eat."

****

Callie moved through the cabin, pushing the food cart from the front of the plane toward the middle. Prepackaged dinners, heated in the microwave in the rear galley, filled the air with mixed aromas. None smelled particularly good.

The lights were back on, and while some had slept during the film, others became restless and wandered the aisles. The seatbelt sign remained unlit and the restriction un-imposed. She didn't want turbulence but prayed the captain would switch the buckled icon back on to ease the congestion. She stopped at the back of a man blocking her way. "Excuse me, sir. If you could please take your seat, I'm about to start serving dinner."

The lanky gentleman backed into his seat and plopped down.

Consulting the stack of orders completed by the passengers, Callie distributed dinners per choice.

"This isn't mine." A deep voice drew her lowered gaze up from reading. She hadn't realized her location. Those Montana blues pierced her soul again.

She gazed from the label to the order form and then back to him. "I apologize. You ordered the Mexican entrée." Her knees weakened as she exchanged the dinners and handed him the correct one. Managing a smile, she reached past him and gave the original meal to the man in the next seat. Mr. Handsome's breath warmed the back of her arm.

She straightened and assumed a business-like posture. "Enjoy," she said, without exchanging glances again, and rolled her cart forward.

When she reached aisle nine, D seat was empty. She tapped her toe and waited for the dark-haired man to return. In less than a minute, he appeared from the bathroom, rubbing his hands as though they might still be damp from washing. His stony expression didn't waver when they exchanged glances. Callie backed away to give him room to seat himself, and in the flurry of movement, his jacket parted enough to reveal what looked like a gun. Her breath seized.

Remain calm. The number one safety motto drilled into her head. But how had he gotten a weapon on board? Though her hands trembled, she managed to finish serving the trays on her cart and returned to the galley. Margo poured drinks in the corner. Callie sidled up to her. "I...I believe one of our passengers has a *gun*."

Margo's head bobbed up. Her eyes widened. "What makes you think that?"

Callie swallowed hard. "The man in 9D—"

Margo sidestepped behind Callie and leaned around the corner. Callie yanked her back. "Don't look! We don't want to make him suspicious."

Her friend's brow arched. "Which man?"

"Dark, icy eyes. Not at all friendly." Callie grabbed the passenger manifest and ran her finger down the list of names. "Kenneth Shalib." She raised her gaze. "Oh, my God, what if he's a terrorist or something?"

Margo's throat pulsed with a hard swallow. "We remain calm and don't panic. Are you even certain you saw a gun?"

Callie wrung her hands. "W...well, not really. I

thought I saw—"

"You *thought*?" Margo rolled her eyes. "It was probably a cell phone or a…a day planner. You certainly can't accuse a man of carrying a weapon because you don't like the way he looks."

"Shush. You don't have to be so loud. Keep your voice down or everyone will hear." Callie leaned back and glanced into the cabin. Everything remained calm except her stomach. Her cheeks warmed at acting like such a ninny.

Margo went back to pouring drinks.

Callie leaned on the counter and hung her head. "This isn't how I planned my first day on the job. You're probably right about the cell phone or whatever, but what if he is carrying a gun?"

Margo didn't look up. "All you can do is keep an eye on him, and if he does anything the least bit suspicious, we'll report him to the—"

A buzzer sounded. Callie nodded. "I'll get that, and," she took a deep breath, "I'll remain panic free. If not, you can put a parachute on my back and push me out the door." She chuckled, but visions of jumping from thirty thousand feet made her queasy. Her palms dampened.

Making her way up the aisle, Callie fixed a smile on her face, released the lamp above the elderly lady's head and gazed down at her. "What can I do for you, ma'am?"

"Could I please get a cup of hot tea with a little honey?" Aging eyes peeked up from beneath bangs of white.

"Tea, I can handle, but I'm not sure we have honey. Will sugar do, if not?"

"That's fine, dear. These old bones just need something to warm them."

"May I get you a blanket?" Callie asked.

"That would be splendid. You're such a sweet girl…remind me of my Rebecca. May she rest in peace." The woman's gaze turned teary.

At a loss for words, Callie pulled a flannel square from the stack in the overhead bin and spread it across the old woman's lap. "I'll be right back with your tea."

Returning to the galley, Callie filled a Styrofoam cup with hot water and dangled a tea bag over the side. The aroma of the darkening brew spiraled up in a cloud of steam. As expected, she found no honey, so grabbed two sugar packets from her serving tray.

Margo returned with her drink tray empty. "I never realized how thirsty people get when they fly." She laughed. "My feet are killing me already."

"Mine too. And so far, this isn't turning out to be my dream job. I've just been compared to a lady's dead daughter." Callie grimaced. "And, I can't turn off the feeling in my gut that tea isn't the only think brewing on this flight. I feel danger in the air. Something about the man in 9D makes the hair on the back of my neck stand on end."

Margo gave a dismissing wave. "I think you have new job jitters. Maybe you should consider asking one of the aft stewardesses to switch with you if that guy makes you so nervous."

Callie shook her head. "I couldn't do that. How embarrassing. I'll be fine, don't worry. Besides, you're right. I'm probably over-anxious about performing well. I've always been a bit of a perfectionist." She picked up her tray. "I need to deliver this tea. Be right back."

Margo grabbed a garbage bag. "I'll pick up the trash. Everyone should be finished eating by now.

* * * *

Taking advantage of a brief respite, the two sat in their jump seats. Callie's butt had barely touched the cushion when a buzzer sounded, and a light shone over row nine. She heaved a heavy sigh and started to rise. Margo touched her arm. "I can get that if you'd like."

"No, I'll do it. He's in my section, and I need to face my fears." She released a loud breath.

Callie slogged down the aisle with feet like lead. Resetting the service light, she fixed him with a faux smile. "How may I help you, sir?"

Those same stony eyes gazed up at her. His narrowed lips, his angular nose, thick brows—she pictured him as a villain in a movie although beneath his seemingly cold exterior, he wasn't bad looking.

"I'd like coffee, please."

"Yes, sir. Would you like milk and sugar?" She maintained her composure and professional attitude.

"Black." His hand slid into his jacket's breast pocket.

Callie's heart seized.

The man withdrew a packet of sweetener and waggled it in the air. "I carry my own."

She released a pent up breath. "Oh, I…I see that. I'll be right back with your coffee."

* * * *

With less than two hours left of the flight, blankets and pillows passed out, hungers sated and thirsts quenched, Callie sat in the jump seat next to Margo. "Whew, I'm beat. I don't think I want to sign up for another trans-Atlantic flight anytime soon. I'd rather do one or two short jaunts in the U.S."

"Oh, I don't know," Margo said. "I've never been to Europe, so this gives me an opportunity to see more of the world. We'll have a twelve-hour layover in England. Home of the Beatles, you know."

"I never was a big Beatle fan, but I *am* anxious to see Britain. She locked her gaze on the cowboy whose big, black hat rested over his face. "I'm more a country girl." Callie chuckled and turned to Margo. "I'm going to take a potty break. Be right back."

Secured inside the restroom, Callie stared at her reflection. Slight dark circles ringed her brown eyes, and her lip color had long ago worn off. She splayed her fingers through her feather-cut blonde hair, plumping it around her face, before fishing inside her pocket for her lipstick. She applied another coat of red and pinched her cheeks. "Not bad for so many hours on the go," she muttered, then washed her hands and stepped outside. She came face to chest with a familiar shirt and gasped as she gazed up into the eyes of Troy Willows.

"I'm next," he said.

She smiled and stepped to the side. He disappeared behind the closed door, and her breathing slowed. What was it about that man that made her feel like a schoolgirl?

She sat back down next to Margo. "I can't wait to get back on the ground. I thought training was tough—"

"Excuse me." Troy Willows towered over the two women. "I wonder if you might help me. I've cut myself somehow." He held up a finger dotted with blood.

Remembering her first aid rules and eager to assist, Callie sprung to her feet. "I'll get you a bandage, but you'll have to return to your seat. Federal rules state no one can loiter in the galley area."

The good-looking man acted as though he hadn't heard her. He cupped his finger, now bleeding heavier, and flicked an urgent glance. "Can you at least get me a cloth before I bleed all over my clothes?"

"Of course." She stepped around him, catching movement from the side of her eye. The man from 9D headed toward the front. Oh, my God, the terrorist was coming to take control. Her heart pounded so loud she imagined everyone could hear it.

Callie grabbed a small towel from the sink area. "Here, Mr. Willows." She shoved the terrycloth at him. "If you'll return to your seat, I'll bring the first aid kit to you." She held her breath, praying the scary passenger only planned to use the washroom. Troy Willows wrapped the towel around his hand and stepped aside so Kenneth Shalib could pass, but Shalib paused in the galley area and swept an assessing gaze over her and her bleeding patient.

Margo rose and stood between the two men. "Excuse me, gentlemen. Both of you need to clear the area at once."

Shalib slipped his hand into his jacket, and a scream crept up Callie's throat. The sound lodged behind a lump of fear. With his free hand, Shalib shoved Margo aside and pulled out a silver revolver. Callie's body shivered, and her legs went limp. Blackness shrouded her as her scream died on her lips.

* * * *

"Are you all right?" Someone patted her cheeks and spoke with a deep, thick accent.

Callie opened her eyes and saw the man from 9D hunkering next to her. Above him, a white blur cleared, and she focused on the shirt and epaulettes of the Captain. The white-haired pilot stared down at her. "Yes, Ms. Corwin, are you okay?"

"W…what happened?" With the dark passenger's help, Callie sat up and rubbed her forehead. Panic pulsed through her. "Where's Margo?" She shrugged free of Shalib's grasp, her gaze searching for her friend. Margo stood next to the captain, looking perfectly fine.

"Cal, you hit your head pretty hard. Are you sure you're okay?" Margo knelt and patted Callie's arm.

"I'm confused is all. W…wha—" Troy Willows sat handcuffed and shackled to the front seat. She turned a raised brow to her co-worker.

"You'll have quite a story to tell about your maiden voyage." Margo laughed. "It seems Mr. Willows here feigned his injury to get his hands on a knife from the galley. He had plans to hijack the plane to France since he's wanted for bank robbery and looking for a new home. Mr. Shalib, an Air Marshall, was assigned to make sure we got safely to our destination. So, I guess you were right when you said you saw a gun."

Callie's cheeks heated. She'd been anything but right in making a wrong assumption of someone based solely on their looks. While acting so giddy over a handsome cowboy, she'd lost sight of her good sense.

She attempted to stand, and Kenneth Shalib helped her to her feet, steadying her. She turned and faced him. "I'm so sorry I misjudged you, but when you slapped my hand away—"

He smiled, and his face softened. His icy exterior

melted. "I'm sorry for that, but I was referring back to a text message with the passenger's name. I couldn't risk you seeing it."

"But your accent…"

"I was born abroad, but I'm an American citizen." His eyes twinkled.

"Will you forgive me for being such a fool and thinking you were the bad guy?"

He winked. "Only if you'll have dinner with me in London and let me show you around the city."

Margo poked her head between them. "Before you two start your sight-seeing venture, we still have to ready this plane for landing."

The captain nodded and returned to the cockpit.

Callie dipped her chin and smiled. "Yes, Mr. Shalib, I'd be delighted to dine with you." She took his arm and turned him toward the aisle. "But please return to your seat now and buckle up. I see the Captain has just turned on the seat-belt sign."

After a last pass through the cabin, Callie took her seat and adjusted her shoulder harness. When she looked up, she locked gazes with Troy Willows. He didn't look quite so handsome sporting his new chains. She iced him with a stare. Because of his charm, she'd joined those who judged a book by its cover, but never again. After surviving this fiasco, she was prepared for anything—well almost.

The End

A Wing and a Prayer

Joy's Revelation

Fresh from her shower, Joy Garrett stood naked in front of the mirror and fingered the inch-long scar just below her navel. The surgery causing it had been performed when she was only ten months old. She'd forgotten the reason her mother gave for the operation, but the resulting jagged line, although small, marred Joy's otherwise flawless torso and irked her. She worked out. Had to. Anyone who wanted to keep Scott Porter on a short leash had to look their best.

Wrapped in terrycloth, she went into the bedroom. Her heart pounded with anticipation of the evening ahead— her first cocktail party and introduction to Scott's co-workers. She planned to make this an evening he'd never forget.

She slipped into her black bra and thong underwear, then removed her dress from the hanger on the closet door. Thankfully those dreadful panty hose of old were passé these days as were those annoying half or full slips. "The less the better," Joy mumbled.

The plastic bag, with the retail store's name emblazoned across it, crackled as she removed it. Annoying static plastered it to her hand. She peeled the cloying cellophane away, wadded it, and flung it into the trash. Visions of her luscious date ran through her mind: Dark hair, eyes bluer than the sky, tall…and those shoulders— broad enough to make other guys envious. "Scott Porter." His name dripped from her tongue like water from melting ice as she shimmied into her dress. Thoughts of him turned her stomach fluttery even though they'd been seeing one another for the past six months. She hoped to marry him one day. Of course, her dreams hinged on him asking.

She had one year left to complete her master's degree and still lived at home. A part-time job didn't offer the luxury of an apartment. Sharing the rent with a roommate was an option, but she was holding out for something better. Yep, someday she'd be Joy Ann Porter if she had her way. She warmed at the thought of greeting each morning in Scott's arms.

Tonight, she wanted to look her best. Her red and black ankle-length gown fit like someone had designed it especially for her, and surprisingly enough, she'd even won over her mother in their debate about the neckline. She chuckled, recalling the scene in the store when she'd stepped out of the dressing room.

"That's quite a dress, Joy, but are you sure it's right for you. It's so…so low cut." As Mom always did when worried about something, she clicked a fingernail against her bottom teeth.

"*Mother*, I'm twenty-four or have you forgotten? Besides, I hardly think I want to make a grand entrance wearing a print button-up like Grandma would choose."

Mom sighed and flashed a weak smile. "I suppose I'll never get used to seeing you as an adult. Here you are almost a college graduate, and I still think of you as my little girl."

"I'll always be your little girl because I'm your only child, but I love this dress so…please Mom, say you'll buy it for me."

The price tag on the red-trimmed ebony gown

represented most of Joy's part-time waitressing paycheck, but surveying herself in the mirror showed the sexy little number was well worth the money. Pressing her palms together, she turned pleading eyes to her mother. "I promise as soon as I get my check from Steak n Bake, I'll reimburse you…every penny."

Mom bought the dress. Now Joy had only to put her marriage proposal plan into action.

She straightened a spaghetti-strap, stepped into her black high-heels, and smiled at her reflection. Scott was bound to notice how the clingy material accentuated her best attributes—ones she planned to use on him tonight.

Back in the bathroom, a quick touch up with the flat-iron repaired the places where her hair threatened to spring back into those despised spirals. Why couldn't she have nice straight hair? Unruly curls made her appear much younger, except for those she planned. Slim tendrils framed her face while the remaining locks, held tight in a stylish clip, hung down her bare back.

She sighed, content God had gifted her with good features, natural blonde tresses, and a fat-free body, but wrestled with guilt for whining over something as petty as curls. Picking up a can of spray, she added another spritz for good measure. The style didn't have to hold long; just until she made her appearance at the party. What she had planned for later would muss her hair anyway.

Returning to the bedroom, she stood in front of the full-length mirror again. "Hmm, not bad for a gal who usually wears jeans and a T-shirt." She made a full circle, watching herself all the way around, and then gave herself a playful slap on the fanny. If Scott didn't approve of his date, there was something seriously wrong.

She reached for her beaded clutch and silky wrap, then snapped her fingers—Scott's boutonnière. The red rosebud surrounded with sprigs of baby's breath was in the refrigerator downstairs. Whether he brought a corsage or not, she wanted him to have a touch of color to match her dress. This was a first experience for her. Did women even wear corsages to these events? She went downstairs.

Waiting, she flicked on the stereo and set the dial to a slow song matching her romantic mood. Mom and Dad were out for dinner and the house was too quiet without the familiar sound of a game show on the TV. She sat on the sofa's edge, but fidgeted. Pulling her long skirt aside, she stood and paced. Tonight had to be perfect. Scott had just graduated with his MBA and landed his dream job. She planned to give him the most precious gift she could think of—her virginity. Pausing in front of the mirror over the fireplace, she adjusted a stray hair and moistened her lips. Thoughts of what was to come set butterflies lose in her belly. She clutched her midsection and took a long breath.

Holding Scott at arm's length the past months hadn't been easy. He was a normal male with needs. Boy, she'd heard that often enough. So far, he'd respected her morality plea and contented himself with kisses and heavy breathing. Oh, he tried an occasional stray touch here and there, but Joy, being blessed with her mother's admonishing glare, kept him in tow.

She paced for a few minutes then perched on the arm of the overstuffed sofa. Joy smoothed her skirt and tapped an impatient foot. A knock sounded. She answered the door, praying to see a gaping mouth and wide eyes.

Scott rapped his knuckles against the weathered wood and then smoothed a hand down his tie. The door opened. Standing in the illumination from the lamp behind her, Joy's beauty stole the breath from his lungs. He inhaled and cast an assessing gaze at the vision before him. He'd never seen her in anything other than casual attire. And this? Her dress enhanced curves he'd only felt and exposed cleavage he wanted to bury his face in.

The crotch of his trousers tightened. "Wow, you look awesome." He stepped inside.

Her ruby lips parted, but before she could speak, he snared the back of her head and brought her mouth to his. Waltzing her backwards, he closed the door with a kick of his heel and tightened his embrace. Their tongues met in an explosion that jarred his insides. God, he wanted her, now more than ever.

Joy leaned away. "Whoa, that's a nice greeting, but you're mussing my do." She smiled and wriggled free from his embrace, patting the sides of her hair. "It's a good thing Mom and Dad are out."

"I'm sorry, sweetheart. I don't know what came over me. I think it has something to do with how sexy you look." His gaze locked on the mounds of her creamy white breasts. "No parents at home, eh?" He reached to snare her again, but she sidestepped his attempt.

"Don't we have a party to attend?"

He released a sigh and straightened his jacket. "You're right. Are you ready?"

"Just let me grab something real quick." She dashed into the kitchen and returned with a single rose bud and stick pin. "I got you a boutonnière."

"What a dunce?" He slapped the side of his head. "Was I supposed to get you a corsage?" He'd shown up empty-handed instead of planning ahead and being as thoughtful as she obviously was.

She shrugged. "I wasn't sure. The last time I had one was at my senior prom, so I'm pretty sure a corsage isn't a requirement for a cocktail party. I wanted you to have a splash of red to match my dress." She stepped closer and attached the bud to his lapel.

Her subtle perfume assaulted his senses, but if he nuzzled her neck now, he'd never let go. Instead he gazed down at his newly acquired deco. "Looks nice. Thanks, babe."

"You're welcome." She grabbed her purse and wrap from the arm of the couch. "Let's go. I'm so looking forward to tonight."

He opened the door, made sure it was locked behind him and followed her onto the porch. "Don't get your hopes up. I doubt the party will be very exciting. I'm thinking I'll probably be fighting guys off my date all evening."

"Oh, trust me." She faced him, her voice a purr. "You'll find it a lot more exciting than you expect."

Her warm breath, smelling of mint toothpaste, washed over him like a summer rain before she spun and walked away. He stood on the porch and pondered her meaning.

"Are you coming?" She stood next to the passenger door.

Scott hurried down the walk, key in hand, and unlocked the door. "What did you mean by more exciting than I expect?"

She slid inside and smiled up at him. "I'm not telling. You'll just have to wait and see."

* * * *

With only she and Scott left at the round white-draped table, Joy leaned closer. His aftershave intoxicated her, and visions of how to present her surprise jumbled in her head.

He'd been right about the party. After introductions and dinner, the crowd waned before the band started. Of those remaining, few danced to music aimed at a much younger crowd. The majority of people attending were older and used their children as an excuse to escape the boredom.

"Would you like to dance again?" Scott's invitation sounded apologetic.

She ran her finger around his ear lobe. "I have a better idea."

His eye's widened. "Really? What?"

She fished in her purse and pulled out a card key. She wiggled the plastic square in front of him. "This opens a door to room 351 at the Capri Motel. Care to join me there?"

His chair legs squealed against the tiled floor as he bolted to his feet. "Would I? You must have been reading my mind."

"I don't think so." She chuckled. "I've had this planned for two weeks."

Scott pulled out her chair and offered his arm. "I'm ready when you are."

On the ride to the motel in Scott's Corvette, Joy stared out the window at the myriad of lights among the boulevard. She relied on music from the radio to fill the conversation gap. Her nerves churned in her stomach like an electric mixer, and her earlier aggressive attitude now turned to cowardice. Talking the talk was much easier than walking the walk, as the cliché she recalled ran through her mind. She knew nothing about sex except what she'd seen in movies and read in romance novels. Putting her femininity on the line frightened the hell out of her. What had she been thinking?

"You're being awful quiet." Scott reached over and caressed her bare thigh. The slit in her dress had hiked up when she slid into the seat, and his fingers felt cool on her bared flesh.

Looking at him, she flashed a weak smile. "Just thinking about what I have planned for us."

"And what would that be?" One dark brow arched.

"Oh, I think you have a hint, given we're going to a motel. I'm just not so sure that you're going to truly appreciate my gift to celebrate your graduation and new job." She bit her knuckle.

"Are you kidding? I've been dying to share your bed for months."

She stared into her lap, her moist palms clasped together there. "Getting a motel and seducing you sounded like a perfect idea until right now."

"What changed?"

"I just realized how inexperienced I am." She glanced up, her chest tight. "What if I disappoint you?"

He took his eyes off the road for a split second and glanced at her. "I love you, Joy. You won't disappoint me. I've done a few turns around the romance track, but I'm not a gigolo by any means. We'll learn to pleasure one another together. Deal?"

She covered his hand with hers. "Just as long as you take it slow. I've heard having sex the first time hurts like heck." She grimaced at the thought.

"Well, I wouldn't know." He drew his hand back to the steering wheel and flicked on the turn signal. "I've never been intimate with a virgin before." His gaze flashed on her again. Oncoming headlights sparkled in his eyes. "See, that makes your gift even more special."

The flashing neon motel lights cast darting colors throughout the car's interior and lent some class to the low-rate special she'd booked. The place had looked much cheesier in broad daylight but the cost fit her budget. Joy swallowed hard, feeling a lump growing in her throat. She exhaled a loud breath and opened the car door. "Well, here we are."

* * * *

Using the card key, Scott opened the door. Unlike Joy, his smile didn't dim at the overwhelming cigarette odor or the worn floral bedspread. The coffee pot looked totally out of place on the credenza next to the television and close to the small refrigerator in the corner that came to life in a spasm of wheezing. The low wattage bulb overhead showed management's attempt to conserve energy. Everything about the room screamed "cheap."

Joy stood in the doorway clutching her handbag. A little voice in her head advised her to run. Her stomach churned. Why hadn't she checked out the room beforehand? This certainly wasn't where she imagined her first experience at lovemaking.

"C'mon." Scott tugged her inside and shut the door.

She shook her head. "This is ridiculous." Tears welled in her eyes.

He gathered her into an embrace and peered down his perfect nose. "It's not the Ritz, but it's not that bad. I've been in worse."

Was that supposed to make her feel better? It didn't. She pulled away. "Why don't we just forget my idea for now? Honestly, Scott, I feel horrible for bringing you to such a dive." She stared at the ratty carpet.

Snaring her back, he cupped her chin and forced her to meet his gaze. "You could take me to the local garbage dump, and I'd still feel like I was in heaven as long as you were there."

Before she could protest again, he kissed her, probing at her lips. She drew his tongue into her mouth, sagging against him. His taste, the feel of his arms around her…she couldn't deny him a thing.

Scott waltzed her backwards until her legs bumped against the mattress. Without breaking his embrace, he lowered her onto the bed and stretched out next to her. Resting his head in his palm, he leaned on one arm and gazed into her eyes. "You're the most beautiful woman in the world."

The ambiance lost importance. Her focus was Scott. Passion burning in her belly, she smiled and splayed her fingers along the corded muscles on his neck. "Have I told you how much I love you?"

Her gasp sounded in the silence when he lowered the strap of her dress and caressed her breast. Her nipples hardened, sending a jolting impulse to the juncture of her thighs. Usually this was where she pushed him away and called a halt to any further foreplay, but not tonight. Tonight was about surrendering herself totally to the man she loved—the man who loved her.

* * * *

Sated, Joy remained stretched across the bed next to Scott. Their clothes lay in a heap on the floor. On his back, Scott's labored breathing began to ease. He took a large inhalation and released the air in a loud sigh. "Oh, that was wonderful." He turned his head and smiled. "I have no idea why you were worried. I think you might teach me a thing or two." His wilting manhood rested on his belly. She tried not to stare.

Feeling the chill in her afterglow, Joy pulled up the sheet and covered her nudity. Strange, she didn't feel self-conscious or awkward. Instead, she reveled in knowing Scott had definitely enjoyed her gift. She rolled toward him and wove her fingers through his chest hair. "I thought it was pretty awesome too."

"Did I hurt you, at all?" He caressed her cheek.

"For only a fleeting moment, but then…"

His penis, hard again, poked against her leg. She'd never really seen one except in pictures and marveled at the amazing tricks of the male anatomy. Moments ago, with his seed spent inside the condom, his manhood turned soft. She sensed the change almost immediately, but now his roaming hands and seducing gaze proved he was ready for seconds.

This time there was no pain. What she'd thought was an orgasm hadn't come close. How one's heart stood the strain of ecstasy's pinnacle was beyond her. Her pulse thudded in her ears and her limbs felt rubbery. This was what she'd been passing up? Never again, though she feared if they made love a third time, she might not survive. Had anyone ever been loved to death?

Scott slung his legs over the bed's edge and sat. He raked his fingers through his mussed hair and glanced back at her. "And I though the gift wrapping was superb."

She chuckled. "Are you saying I did good?"

"Good?" He grinned. "Any better and I might have to marry you just to keep you in my bed."

Marry! The mention jolted through her like an earthquake. She hoped he might mention his intentions, but not joke about them. Her good mood faded along with her hopefulness. She pulled the sheet up to her chin and stared at the stained ceiling tiles.

"Care to join me in the shower?" Scott stood and faced the bed, unfazed by his nudity.

"No thanks," she mumbled. "I think I'll just rest a bit if you don't mind."

He ambled into the bathroom. The sound of running water sliced the silence, followed by the sliding of the shower curtain against the metal rod. Tears burned the back of Joy's eyes. Had she just become the "cow" that gave away the proverbial milk? Except for the superb lovemaking, this evening had not played out the way she envisioned.

While he hummed merrily in the shower, she rose and dressed. Standing at the mirror over the dresser, she attempted to repair her tousled hair. Scott came out of the bathroom wrapped in a towel, his hair wet and his chest glistening. He stood behind her and snaked his arms around her waist, resting his chin on her shoulder. "Ah, you're dressed. Does this mean our evening is over?"

She swallowed the lump in her throat. "I have the early shift in the morning."

A water droplet fell from his hair and drizzled down her chest. She wiped it away and turned. "I'd love to stay longer, but I really need to get some sleep."

He backed away, hands raised in surrender. "Okay,

I'll get dressed, but you're cutting into my surprise now."

She cocked her head. "What surprise?"

"I expected to be dressed when I did this, but I can't wait a minute longer." He dropped to one knee and took her hand. "Joy Garrett, would you do me the honor of becoming my wife?"

She widened her eyes. "I-I… Of course I will." Her mouth gaped.

Scott released her hand and inched the short distance to his jacket. He produced a small black box and returned to the spot where he proposed.

A loud gasp escaped her lips when he opened the box, and she beheld a large emerald-cut diamond.

He took hold of her hand again and slipped the ring onto her finger. "I hope you don't mind a long engagement. I want you to have the wedding of your dreams, but I want to make sure me and my job are as great a fit as it seems. We'll have it all, babe: a house, the picket fence, maybe even children someday."

"Oh, Scott." She yanked on his hand and brought him to his feet. "I love you so much, and I'll wait just as long as it takes."

Her lips met his in a long, delving kiss. She tightened her arms around his neck while her soon-to-be title ran through her mind—Mrs. Scott Porter.

* * * *

Sitting on the edge of the bed, Joy bent and tied the laces on her tennis shoes. She stood and gave one last glance at the mirror over her bureau—good enough for serving burgers and fries.

The months had passed quickly. In December, at Christmas dinner, she and Scott had announced they would marry in June. The thought of her pending nuptials made her smile. Working, going to school, spending stolen nights in her fiancé's arms, and checking things off her list of things to do for the wedding helped the days pass in a blur. According to the clock on her nightstand, she had a whole hour before starting her shift at the restaurant.

Dressed in her faded uniform, Joy came downstairs. "Hey, Mom."

Her mother, in her rocking chair, looked up from the newspaper she held. One brow arched.

"Do you have any idea where my birth certificate is? I'm going to need it to get my passport. Scott is planning on a honeymoon in Paris. I'm so excited."

Her mother folded the paper and laid it aside. Her throat wobbled with a hard swallow. "Oh, dear, I haven't seen that certificate since I enrolled you in Kindergarten. Maybe you two should plan to visit someplace right here in the United States. There are some lovely honeymoon sites…like Niagara Falls, Las Vegas…how about New York City? You could even see a Broadway play."

Joy shook her head. "They all sound nice, but Scott is intent on taking me to Europe. He's been there before as an Air Force brat and wants to go back."

"W-well, I'll look for it while you're at work.

"I'd appreciate that." Worry still plagued her. "I'm going to love being a June bride but that gives us only two months." She knelt next to her mother's chair. "Do you think we can pull off a wedding in that amount of time?"

"We'd better. The invitations you had printed arrived yesterday. I put them on your dresser. Did you see them?"

"Yes, they turned out even more beautiful then I imagined, but I still have so much to do. Working is interfering with my organizational skills." She smiled.

"Honestly, Joy, you've taken care of the lion's share. The venue and the minister are scheduled. You've invited friends to be your attendants and decided on the country club for your reception. Of course, you have to take care of dresses for you and your wedding party, and Scott has to reserve tuxes for his best man and the groomsmen, but other than table decorations and the cake, what needs to be done?"

Joy stood. "Oh, I can't think about it right now. I have to get moving or I'll be late." She bent and kissed her mother's cheek. "I'll see you later this evening."

"Have a good day, dear."

Joy paused at the door. "Don't forget to look for my birth certificate."

* * * *

The sunshine beaming through her bedroom window woke Joy. She uncurled into a big stretch then languished in bed, realizing it was Saturday and her day off.

"Get up, lazy bones," she mumbled. "You have appointments to meet: a gown fitting, cake samples to taste, and maybe even a pedicure." She threw back the covers and stood. Donning her robe, she wandered into the hallway and downstairs, in search of coffee.

Her mother stood at the counter, her hands deep in soapy water.

"Mornin' Mom." Joy sidled up next to her, opened the cupboard, and snared a cup.

"You're up earlier than I expected. You were out pretty late with Scott last night."

Joy poured coffee with one hand and stifled a yawn with the other. "Ohhh, I have so much to do today, but we did have a wonderful time last night."

She wondered how her mother would react if she knew they'd made love on the beach. Warmth pulsed through Joy at the memory. Although she had no prior experience, she couldn't imagine anyone being better than Scott in arousing her passion.

"You're going to have your gown fitted, right?" Her mother's voice pulled Joy's attention back.

"O-oh…yes, and trying to find the right veil. I didn't like any of the ones the shop had in stock. The manager said they were getting some new ones in this week. By the way, did you happen to find my birth certificate."

Her mother drained the sink, dried her hands and caressed Joy's cheek. "You'll need something old, something new, something borrowed, and something blue." She changed the subject, so clearly she hadn't found the paper Joy needed. "You know what? I think you'd look stunning in the veil I wore when I married your father. I also have a garter with a touch of blue if you're interested."

"I'd love to see them. You aren't upset that I wanted my own gown, are you?"

"Not at all. Let's go up and rifle through my cedar chest."

Joy followed her mom upstairs puzzled why wanting a birth certificate was such an issue. Maybe Mom had just misplaced it. The attic door creaked open, releasing a musty odor when they stepped inside. Sunshine filtered through the glass panes below the eaves, allowing light enough to see. Boxes marked "Christmas decorations" filled one corner of the storage area, while a dressmaker's dummy, an old wing-backed chair, and more stacked boxes sat nearby. The cedar chest, its lid coated with dust, filled a space along the far wall.

Anticipation tingled through Joy. "Oh my gosh, I haven't been up here for years…not since I was ten and discovered this was where Santa hid my gifts." She giggled.

"I remember that." Her mother clicked her tongue against her teeth. "You spoiled our surprises that year." She pulled the chair closer, sat and opened the chest.

Anxious, Joy knelt and waited for her mother to remove the inner shelf and reveal what treasures lay inside.

* * * *

Joy lost track of time. They'd been upstairs for hours—strolling down memory lane. They'd found the veil and garter all right, but so much more: Joy's baby book, pictures of her mom and dad's wedding, crocheted and knitted pieces handed down from her grandmother, a child's christening gown. Joy had no idea her mother had saved so much of her past.

The items covered the floor, and they'd almost reached the bottom. Downstairs, the phone rang. Her mother rose. "I'd better get that. I'm expecting a call from the caterer." She turned and disappeared out the door.

Joy continued digging. Beneath an old quilt, she found the family Bible and lifted it out. Sitting Indian style, she rested the large book in her lap and flipped open the cover. Inside, she found loose newspaper clippings of family obituaries, wedding announcements, and an entire article about the Pearl Harbor bombing. The written record of family births and deaths held no entries. Joy shook her head and smiled. Mom never got around to making notes, as evidenced by the empty pages in Joy's baby book. The woman definitely had a penchant for collecting things, though.

Near the back of the book, Joy found a folded paper. She straightened it and blinked. In her hands, a birth certificate dated the day she was born, but it wasn't hers. Her fingers trembled as a fearful thought shuddered through her. "Who in the hell…"

"Joey Andrew Garrett." Joy read the name. Born the same day, same hospital, and same doctor her mother had mentioned. But a male child? Joy touched her abdomen—the scar. A million questions roared in her mind, but none she wanted to ask. The answers might be too frightening. She stuffed the certificate back where she found it, put the Bible beneath the quilt, and then placed everything except the veil and garter back inside the chest. She lowered the lid and stood, her pulse pounding in her head. What did it mean? "Oh, my God, I'm a freak." She covered her face with her hands and fought the tears stinging the back of her eyes.

Joy pulled herself together. Carrying the gauzy veil and silken garter, she closed the attic door and hurried downstairs.

She collided with her mother. "Oh, I was just on my way back up. Everything's fine with the catering. I got everything you wanted."

"That's great, Mom." Joy averted her gaze. "I've got to get dressed or I'm going to be late for my fitting."

"Did you finish going through everything?" her

mother asked.

"Yes, and I put everything away. It was definitely a very…very interesting morning."

* * * *

The scenery whizzed by as Joy sped toward the bridal shop. She kept her eyes on the road while driving, but her mind drifted to unpleasant places. How could she marry Scott now? Her knuckles whitened on the steering wheel. Didn't he deserve to know everything about the person he was about to wed? How would she tell him, and worse, how would he react?

Hard to believe that for twenty-four years her parents had kept such an important secret from her. More so, why? She'd heard about babies born with the genitalia of both genders…hermaphrodites, she thought they were called, but….her?

Tears blurred her eyes. She steered the car to the side of the road and stopped. With the gearshift in park, she dipped her chin and massaged the tension headache growing between her eyes. How could this be? She'd always felt like a girl, and in her memory, had always been a girl. In fact, people always commented on how feminine and delicate she was as a child. Evidently the doctor didn't see it that way when they filled out her birth certificate.

Lost in a sea of emotions, she wondered what to do. Starting marriage with a lie…especially one this big, was not her choice. She'd rather lose Scott than dishonor him. Fishing in her purse for her cellphone, she found it and dialed the number for the bridal shop.

"Yes, this is Joy Garrett. I have an appointment

with you today, but I'm not going to be able to keep it. I'm sorry."

"Would you like to reschedule," a voice on the other end of the line asked.

"Not at this time. Thank you and I'm sorry for the inconvenience."

After flipping the cover closed, she tossed the phone aside. She twirled her engagement ring around her left finger and surrendered to her feelings. With her hands as a buffer, she pressed her forehead to the steering wheel and sobbed. When she had no more tears to cry, she squared her shoulders, put the car into drive and made a U-turn. All those questions she feared asking now begged for answers, and Mom was going to provide them whether she liked it or not.

* * * *

Joy didn't mean for the door to slam when she walked into the front foyer. Her mother, clad in her apron and flour on her hands, appeared in the kitchen doorway. "Oh, you're back so soon? Did you forget something?"

With a big inhalation, Joy steadied herself. "We need to talk, Mom, and right now."

Her mother's eyes grew wide beneath arched brows. "All right, but you're scaring me with such a serious look on your face and the tone of your voice. Did something happen?"

"Please, can we just sit? I need to ask you something very important…and you need to tell me the truth."

Her mother's mouth drew into a thin line. She

stared at her hands, back at Joy, and then released a loud breath that showed her frustration. "I suppose supper can wait. Let me clean up and I'll be right back."

Joy tossed her purse aside and sat on the edge of the sofa, sorting through her options. Was she doing the right thing in confronting her mother alone? Should she wait for her father…even include Scott in the conversation? Nerves churned her insides into knots. She clasped her hands in her lap and waited. Sand in the Sahara couldn't be any drier than her mouth. She wanted answers and she wanted them now.

"Okay, okay, here I am." Mom appeared, running her just-washed hands down the front of her apron. "Now, what's got you in such a dither?" She sat in her rocker and stared across at Joy.

Joy fluttered her lips with an exhalation. "I don't know where to start. I'm so upset. I think I'm gonna throw up." She rubbed her hand across the furrows in her brow.

"What is it, dear?" Her mother cocked her head. "You've never had a problem talking to me. We've always been able to discuss everything."

"Have we *really*?" Joy leveled an icy stare at her.

"Well, I thought we had a pretty open line of communication between us."

"I thought so, too, *until* I found the secret you've been keeping from me in your cedar chest."

Her mother leaned forward, confusion clouding her eyes. "Whatever are you talking about?"

Joy steeled herself. "Who is Joey Andrew Garrett?"

A gasp sliced the silence. Her mother's mouth gaped.

"Well?"

Tears welled in her mom's eyes and her throat wobbled with a hard swallow. "I-I can't discuss this right now." She bolted to her feet and raced upstairs. The slamming of her bedroom door wobbled the glass panes in the front window.

Stunned, Joy stared at the floor. So much for open communication, but this wasn't over. Someone was going to offer up some answers, and if it had to be her father, then so be it.

Her familiar ringtone sliced the silence. She reached for her pocketbook and retrieved her cellphone. "Hello."

"Hi, Sweetie. Rough day? You sound down."

"You might say that. Can you stop by on your way home from work?"

"I suppose so, but what's going on?" His voice held a nervous tone.

"I wish I knew. I guess we'll find out together when you and my father get here."

* * * *

Joy wavered between crying and pacing the length of her bedroom. Prickled by nervousness, she questioned her decision. Surely Scott would be repulsed by the revelation of the secret. Should she offer back the ring before he demanded it? Images of the beautiful gown she'd picked out floated through her mind and disintegrated into tattered rags. The imagined sunshine on her upcoming wedding day disappeared behind massive thunderclouds. So many calls to make, so many beautiful dreams to cancel.

Tired, she sagged onto the bed and buried her face in her hands. The only positive thought she conjured were the unsent invitations on her bureau. The silence was broken by voices downstairs. Standing, she forced one foot in front of the other and made her way to the living room. Her mother, father, and Scott stood on the braided rug and watched her descend each step.

Scott noticed her and turned his beautiful smile in her direction. "There's my girl." He crossed to the bottom of the staircase and enveloped her into a hug. She glanced over his shoulder at her mother and noted the apprehension in her eyes.

Holding her at arm's length, Scott raised a brow. "Now what's this important news that we all have to share?"

Joy's breath hitched. She cleared her throat. "First, I think we all need to sit."

Her mother and father sat side-by-side in their rocker-recliners. Scott waited until Joy was seated on the sofa and then plopped beside her. The tension in the air hung heavy, and the silence begged to be broken.

Her father leaned forward and rested his arms on his knees. His pensive gaze focused on Joy. "Your mother called me this afternoon and clued me in on what has you so upset and worried."

Joy glanced at her mother and then at Scott. Tears blurred her eyes as she twisted off her engagement ring, placed it in her open palm, and extended it toward him. "Before you ask for this back, I'm offering it to you in order to save face. I'm sure when you hear the truth, you won't feel the same about me."

He folded her fingers over the ring and held them closed. "There is nothing you can tell me that's going to change my love for you."

"I wouldn't bet on it." Her voice cracked. She

looked at her parents while wiping away a tear. "Do you want to tell him or should I?"

Her father reached over and patted her mother's hand. "It's okay, Claire, I'll handle this."

He looked at Joy. "You asked your mother earlier about Joey Andrew Garrett." His protruding Adam's apple bobbed with a swallow. "We made a very difficult decision twenty-four years ago to keep something from you, and now we realize we were wrong. We should have told you when you were old enough to understand."

Scott shrugged. "What am I missing? Who is this Joey?"

Joy dipped her chin and stared into her lap. "I'm afraid it's me. I found my birth certificate in the attic, and I-I was born a boy. Now I know the real reason I have a scar on my abdomen."

"What!" Her mother shouted. "Is that what you think?"

Her father's eyes turned wide. "You couldn't be further from the truth."

Joy wiggled her hand free from Scott's and leaned forward. "How can I be wrong? The birthday, the hospital, the city and state...everything matches when and where I was born."

Her mother dabbed her eyes with a hankie. "Y-you weren't the only child born on that day."

"Huh?" She glanced from her parents, to Scott, and back

"You were a twin," her father added. "Your brother only lived for a few hours. He had a hole in his heart and died before the doctors could operate."

Joy sat in stunned silence for a few seconds and then

hunched her shoulders closer to her ears. "Why didn't you tell me? Here I thought…"

"I suppose if I had been in your place and found something hidden, I might have jumped to the same conclusion. I wanted to tell you today, but hearing his name and remembering his loss was more than I could handle." Her mother screwed her mouth into a frown. "As for the scar…you had a hernia repair when you were very young." She crossed to the sofa, sat next to her daughter and rested her arm on her shoulders. "Can you forgive me—us?"

"Oh, Mom, I'm so relieved, I think I could forgive anything at this moment." The proverbial black cloud of doom that had hovered overhead disappeared. She kissed her mother on the cheek.

Turning to Scott, she dipped her chin and looked through her lashes. "I'm such a dope. Are you sure you don't want your ring back?"

He took the ring from her palm and slipped it back on her finger. "You might be a dope, but you're all mine."

She put her arms around his neck and pulled him close. "I love you with all my heart and I can't wait to be your wife."

Joy raised her eyes. "Thank you, God," she spoke in a whisper, "for making me a girl and letting me live to enjoy this moment. Even more for taking care of my little brother."

The End

Just the Right Fit

Carolyn Farris held an expensive walking shoe in her hand under the guise of inspecting it, but the gaze from the corner of her eye remained fixed on the handsome, mature salesman arranging a display across the room. The heat of his occasional glance served as a magnet, pulling her attention to him. She couldn't ignore him if she tried. He definitely was new—not the kind of hunk a gal forgot.

The prices in this specialty store were far outside her restrictive budget, so she waited until they held a clearance sale. One couldn't put a tag on comfort, yet guilt panged her at the thought of being frivolous with her money when she needed so many other things: new tires, Freon for her car air conditioning, even a new bra. A sale ad had drawn her here today, and this was the first time she'd run across something much more interesting than footwear. Even at sixty-four and long past being a giddy schoolgirl, she hadn't forgotten the feelings of an emotional roller coaster.

Countless years had passed since she'd been on a date, and the urge to flirt gnawed at her, but she'd forgotten how. Back in the day, she would have had no qualms initiating a conversation and exchanging numbers, but her youth had sailed away, leaving her nothing but insecurities from a failed marriage and the string of bum relationships that followed. Early retirement, forced by a situation with an intolerable boss, and the onslaught of legal matters, denied benefits, and health issues had taken a toll on her sanity. Maybe she was crazier than she thought, believing anyone would find her the least bit interesting.

She released a loud sigh and carried the single shoe back to a seat, waiting for service. How could she get so excited over someone she didn't even know? She stared into her lap and prayed for composure from the flush creeping up her neck. Maybe she should've shopped for a bra today instead.

"May I help you?" The timbre of his voice matched the broadness of his shoulders and made her jump. His tall silhouette blocked the light filtering through the front window, and her dipped chin seemed frozen in place.

She forced her head up. "Y-es, I-I…" The words she sought lodged behind a lump in her throat.

"I assume you're holding the shoe you're interested in." His smile dimpled his cheeks and displayed white, even teeth. If they were false, they didn't look it.

An air of charisma hung about him while she felt caught up in a bubble of ridiculousness. She forced a smile and with trembling fingers, handed him the shoe. "Yes, size seven please."

Why in the world did this man have such an effect on her? Could the draw be the splashes of gray at his temples? It couldn't be the slight limp she detected when he walked through the curtain to the storeroom. But there was something—definitely something. She thrummed her fingertips on the chair's arm and fidgeted in her seat, waiting for his return—almost dreading the feelings he stirred and unsure how to handle them.

"Here we go." He appeared through the split material in the doorway with a beige box bearing the familiar logo of the footwear she'd learned to love. With one hand, he hiked up his khaki slacks before kneeling in front of her. He removed her left shoe, his grasp warming her heel when he slipped off her worn pump.

The personal service kept her coming back to the store. Almost no one waited on customers anymore—especially clerks this yummy. Yummy? That word certainly dated her…but he was. She fanned her fingers across her heated face and fixed her gaze on the top of his head—not even a bald spot in his thick brown hair. The man was definitely eye candy, and she wasn't on a diet.

While he slipped on the other walking shoe and tied the laces, Carolyn searched his left hand for a wedding band. His naked finger caused a little squeal to bubble in her throat, but it quickly slid back down when she considered he might be gay. Wouldn't that be just her luck?

"They look very nice." He stood back and flashed that selling smile—anything for a sale, she supposed. "How do they feel?"

"F-fine." She jutted her legs out and stared at her feet. "I like them."

"Perhaps you should walk around the room." He offered his hand and helped her stand. "Make sure they don't pinch those pretty little toes."

She hadn't had tummy butterflies in ages, but he set a flurry loose with a wink of his azure eye. The touch of his palm sent an electric jolt up her arm, and her benign attraction to him turned terminal. How could she sashay across the floor in tennis shoes and a skirt and still look alluring? She craved perfection in his eyes.

Inhaling the manly scent of his aftershave, she smiled up at him and understood why women in ages past swooned. If she did, would he catch her? Not willing to risk injury, she pushed aside the idea of flinging the back of her hand to her forehead and crumpling in his direction.

"I'll take them." She gathered her remaining wits. "This isn't my first pair, so I know they'll fit just fine."

With legs like jelly, she plopped back in the chair and bent to untie the laces.

He knelt again and brushed her hands aside. "Allow me, please."

She leaned back, her spine stiff against the chair, but she tried to strike a sensual pose as she lifted one foot and then the other. After slipping back into her old shoes, she followed him to the cash register, taking in the perfect fit of his trousers against a trim behind and narrow waist.

At the counter, she fished inside her purse for her wallet while he rang up the sale. She couldn't let the moment pass without at least appearing to be interested. But before she worked up the courage, he glanced at her debit card and then back up at her. "So, Ms. Farris, is there a Mr.?"

She bit her lip to stifle her amusement. "Oh, no there isn't. Hasn't been one for many years." Mr. Yummy had opened the door; all she needed to do was walk in. "How about you? Are you married?"

He flashed a sheepish smile. "I am married, but only for about two more weeks; then I'll be a free man. My wife decided to run off with our thirty-five-year-old gardener."

Carolyn fought the urge to reach across and pat his hand—to comfort him and comment on his wife's bad judgment, but she simply shook her head. "I'm sorry to hear that."

Was she really sorry? The old adage, "one person's garbage is another person's treasure," flashed in her mind. What possible flaw could this man have that would cause someone to throw him away? Curiosity chewed on her, but she refused to appear nosy.

He bagged her shoes and handed the parcel across the counter. "I'm happy I could serve you today."

Their hands brushed, and his eyes mellowed. His Adam's apple bobbed with a heavy swallow, and Carolyn assumed he wanted to say something, but he didn't. She accepted the package and backed away from the counter. "Have a nice day, Mr.—"

"Mike…Mike Olson. No need to be so formal."

She smiled. "Then Mike it is. You can call me Carolyn." *Or, you can just call me*, her mind added. Lacking courage, she walked toward the exit, praying he'd summon her back and at least ask for her phone number. He didn't. She paused at the door. "Thank you for your help. It was very nice to meet you."

She walked outside, her stomach sick at her lack of courage. If she possessed one ounce of courage, she'd traipse back inside and at least grab a business card. Sadly, she lacked anything remotely resembling nerve. Momma always said that nice girls sit and wait, so with a sigh, Carolyn walked away.

* * * *

In the car, Carolyn's hands tightened on the steering wheel. Her jaw tensed. Why hadn't she stuck around and chatted a little more? The distinct feeling that he held an interest in her hadn't left since the moment she entered the store. Had she just passed up on the perfect opportunity?

"Crap!" she muttered, one hand reaching to change the radio station to something more soothing than the traffic report. At her age, these opportunities didn't come by often…if ever. Another 'momma-ism' flashed in her head. *Your body may age, but your brain will always be young.* Carolyn chuckled. She still saw herself as twenty, at least until she looked into the mirror. Still, she planned on seeing Mr. Mike Olson again and soon.

She nibbled her bottom lip, scheming all the while. She might be driving the car, but determination drove her. Some way, somehow, she planned a return visit. Would buying another pair of shoes be too obvious?

Carolyn steered the car into her neighborhood, but instead of pulling into her driveway, she continued down the block to her best friend's house. Sally always provided a willing ear, shoulder, or support whenever needed. Carolyn hurried from her red sedan and rapped on Sally's front door.

"Hey, what are you doing here so early in the afternoon?" Sally stood behind the open door, clasping her robe together.

"How come you aren't dressed?"

"Oh, I don't know. Since retiring, I've found it pretty easy to adapt to the comforts of home. Besides," her tone tugged her lips into a frown, "most of my clothes don't fit anymore because I can't keep my head out of the refrigerator."

"Oh, I know the feeling," Carolyn commiserated. "But this is the first time in ages I've seen you with tousled hair and no make-up."

"Well, get used to it. I don't having anything to gussy up for now, unless…" Sally crinkled her brow. "Have I forgotten something we're supposed to do together?"

"No, I just need someone to talk to." Without waiting for an invitation, Carolyn opened the screen and walked inside. She released a loud breath. "Ohhh, I'm so mad at myself I could scream." She sank onto the floral sofa.

Sally closed the door and faced her with an arched brow. She tied the sash at her waist and walked to the kitchen counter. "Coffee?"

"Sure. Put some arsenic in mine." Carolyn clenched her hand into a claw and growled.

"What's wrong?" Sally filled two cups, carried them over to the couch, and set them on the coffee table. She picked up her mug and sat in the adjacent easy chair.

"I met the most handsome and nice man today—"

"And that's what you're angry about?" Sally rolled her eyes and took a sip.

"No! I'm upset because I didn't do anything to encourage him. I know he was interested in me, too. I felt it." The memory of his stare tickled her stomach.

"And where did you meet this Adonis?" Sally put the steaming brew on the coffee table and leaned back.

"In the SAS shoe store. As soon as I walked in, I felt the sparks between us." She picked up her cup and sipped. Bitterness lingered on her tongue.

"So why don't you just go back again?"

Carolyn clucked her tongue against her teeth. "And embarrass myself? I don't want him to think I'm chasing after him."

Sally lifted her cup again. "Well, don't expect me to come up with any ideas. I ran out about thirty years ago." She chuckled and peered over the ceramic rim. "Did you buy the shoes?"

"Yes, so if I go back so soon, he's going to know I'm there just to see him."

"I suppose you're right." Sally stood and carried her

coffee back into the kitchen. "This tastes old. Let me make a fresh pot."

"Don't bother." Carolyn stood. "I'm not really in the mood for coffee anyhow. I'm gonna head home and pout."

Sally walked her to the door. "Call me later and let me know when you're ready for our walk."

"That's it!" Carolyn snapped her fingers and smiled.

* * * *

Soft jazz emanated from Carolyn's car radio. Sally seemed engrossed in the train that clacked along the rails along the frontage road. She turned her gaze on Carolyn. "I'm still not clear on what you expect me to do. I don't need new shoes."

Carolyn flashed a glance. "No one said you had to buy anything. Just act interested."

"Oh, I see. I'm just a pawn in this chess game you're planning." She returned to watching the graffiti-covered freight cars.

"Consider you're helping your best friend find possible romance." She patted Sally's hand. "In your company, I won't look desperate."

"Okay." Sally nodded. "But you owe me big time."

Carolyn's excited heart thudded. She pulled into an open parking spot in front of the store, still rehearsing her scripted dialogue. She took a deep breath. "Well, here we are."

Sally flung her purse strap over her shoulder. "Okay, let's put 'Operation Snare Him' into motion. I've got a nail appointment in two hours."

Her first few steps shaky, Carolyn followed Sally inside. Mike stood behind the counter. He looked up, and her heart quickened. "Hi, remember me?"

His face broadened with a smile. "Of course. I'm happy to see you again." His gaze never left her face.

Carolyn's cheeks heated, and she gestured to her companion. "This is my friend. I told her about my new shoes and your sale, and she *insisted* I bring her by."

Sally's blank stare wandered the store.

Carolyn elbowed her. "Didn't you, Sally?"

Holding her side, Sally grimaced but nodded. "O-oh, yeah. Carolyn was kind enough to drive me here. If you don't mind, I'll just look around." She ambled off toward a display of sandals.

"Let me know if you find something you like," Mike called after her.

Carolyn found it strange she didn't feel awkward. Mike leaned on the counter and began asking questions; the conversation flowed. In the process, she shared with him her living arrangements, how long she'd been single, retired from working for the labor board, and even her age. They discussed the trip he'd taken to Costa Rica, the fact that he'd been a police officer until he retired, his diabetes, and pending hip replacement. Nothing he said made him any less attractive to her. In fact, she appreciated his honest approach to life.

Sally returned to the counter. "Sorry, but I didn't see anything I can't live without."

Carolyn fisted her hand at her side, not wanting her time with Mike to end. But unable to think of a reason to tarry, she again bid him goodbye, lingering just in case he asked for her number. An incoming customer spoiled the moment. Carolyn waved and walked out the door, her shoulders sagging.

She stopped in the parking lot and handed the keys to Sally. "Go wait in the car. I'm not giving up and going home like a cowardly dog with its tail between its legs. I'm going back inside and at least get a business card. Actually, I'm giving him one more chance to show he's interested."

Carolyn stepped back into the air-conditioned store, her eyes taking a moment to adjust from the bright sunlight. She headed for the empty counter and the plastic cardholder just as Mike and the female customer appeared through the stockroom curtains.

A blow to the stomach couldn't have left her more breathless. Carolyn gaped at the pair who walked with their arms around one another. The smiles on their faces and the familiar way they leaned into one another created an awkward situation. There was no way she could make it out the door without being noticed, in fact, Mike's gaze rested on her almost immediately.

"Oh, Carolyn, did you forget something?" He dropped his arm from around the other woman's waist.

"N-not really." Why didn't the ground swallow her up? "Ah... In case my friend changes her mind about needing shoes, I came back for a business card." She took one and fluttered her eyelids at such a lame excuse. Without another word, she ducked out the door and crossed the parking lot to the car. The engine was running and the interior already cool when she slid behind the wheel.

"Well?" Sally looked over with an arched brow. "Did he ask you out?"

Carolyn gripped the steering wheel and banged her head against it. "Noooo. I'm such a fool."

"Why? What happened?"

She turned to Sally. "That woman we passed on the way out seems to be more than a friend. They were in the back room together and looking pretty chummy when they came out. I felt like an idiot."

Carolyn tossed the business card in her purse. "Guess I won't need this." She put the car in reverse and backed out of the parking space, stopping to glance at her friend. "I'm so sorry I talked you into this lame idea. I have no idea when I became so desperate."

* * * *

Carolyn stuffed her breakfast dishes in the dishwasher and started the rinse cycle. She'd dreamed of Mike all night, and now she couldn't think of anything else. Despite the cozy appearance of him with another woman, Carolyn refused to say "uncle." She'd find an excuse to talk to him again. Always up for a challenge, she believed she had as much to offer as the woman in the store. Instead of giving up, she grappled for any method to snare his interest.

The idea of using Sally as a prospective shopper hadn't worked, so what now? Her gaze wandered to the phone. She could call the store, but she'd never asked a man out before. Out of small talk, what would she say? Her mother had drilled into her brain that invitations fell on the man's shoulders, and women who did the asking were brazen. That wasn't the impression she wanted to make on Mike.

She dug in her purse and found his business card. Eyeing the number, she sat at the table and struggled with all the excuses she could use for making the call. Shoe stores were chains, weren't they? Maybe she could call and inquire on behalf of someone who lived out of the area—her sister perhaps. What a brilliant plan! Her mind flashed on prank phone calls she and friends often made during their teenage years, and for a moment she recaptured a piece of her youth.

She walked across the room, retrieved the phone and went back to the table and sat. Her nerves were more frayed than the tie on her old bathrobe.

Carolyn punched in the numbers and listened for the ring. She contemplated hanging up, but determination steeled her nerves. Mike answered, his voice sending shivers through her.

The story she'd concocted seemed legit and put her at ease. "Hi, Mike. This is Carolyn Farris—"

"Oh, Carolyn, how nice to hear from you. I was just thinking about you."

"Are you busy at the moment?" Glad he couldn't see her broad grin at his admission, she stifled a giggle.

"No, actually it's been a very quiet day here. What can I do for you?"

Her mind whirred with all the lovely things he could do for her, but she dared not go there. An image of his female friend flashed through her head, too, but instead of backing down, she fired up her courage and cleared her throat. "I was wondering if your company has a store in Las Vegas. I told my sister about the shoes I bought, and she asked where I got them. I told her I'd check to see if there's a store in her area."

She heard nothing but silence for a moment. Had he figured out her ploy? Any computer savvy person would recommend looking on the Internet, but maybe, just maybe, he wasn't that technologically blessed.

"You know," he finally said. "I'm not sure. I

haven't worked here for long, but I'll be more than happy to check with our corporate office. If you give me your number, I'll call you back tomorrow."

She thanked him for his kindness, gave him her number, and then hung up. She immediately leapt from her chair and did a happy dance. She'd found a way to give him a reason to call her without having looked like that brazen woman Momma warned about. Sweet success. Now all she needed to do was wait and keep reminding herself that she had just as much of a chance with him as anyone else. Maybe.

* * * *

"Crap, I should have given him my cell number." Carolyn berated herself, realizing she had errands to do and couldn't hang by the telephone all day. At least she owned an answering machine. But she couldn't risk him leaving a message. She'd call him. She found the business card in her purse and dialed the number. The voice on the other end didn't sound familiar. "Is Mike there?"

"No, I'm sorry, he hasn't come in yet. Can I take a message?"

Her spirits sagged. "No, no message. Thank you."

She hung up and slunk out to the car. Maybe karma was trying to tell her something.

Carolyn visited the post office, the bank, picked up a few things at the store and returned home. Her heart hitched when she noticed the flashing message light. Unable to wait until she emptied her grocery bags, she slid them onto the counter and pressed the play button.

"Hi, Carolyn. Mike from the SAS store here. There

is a store in Vegas, and here's the number. I hope to see you soon. Have a good day."

She disregarded the number but frowned that he hadn't even hinted at getting together. Perhaps she'd misread him. Desperation most likely made her see interest when all he saw was a possible sale. After all, who would be interested in an old woman? Seized by despair, she bit her bottom lip and fought tears while she put away the things she'd bought. Disappointment sapped her energy, and she headed for the bedroom to take a nap. If she slept, at least she wouldn't dwell on Mike.

Carolyn curled on the bed and sighed. Had she just been playing a game of hope? Was it her looks? According to friends, her professionally highlighted hair hid any traces of gray, and she looked years younger than her actual age. Her figure wasn't as firm as it once was, but she wasn't eligible for the fat lady in the circus position either. Somewhere between knuckling away a few tears and convincing herself she couldn't lose something she never had, she fell asleep.

* * * *

A ringing phone woke her. She opened her eyes and blinked. Very little light filtered through the lace curtains, and the streetlight outside already shined. She'd slept away the afternoon and missed her walk with Sally. Now she'd have to hear all about being consistent with exercise. Fighting off the dreariness, she hurried to the kitchen and answered.

"Carolyn, it's Mike from the shoe store."

She came full awake. "Mike. What a surprise."

"I've fought with myself all day about whether or not to call you. I would really like to invite you out, but I've been so afraid you wouldn't be interested."

"You're kidding?" She'd gone to such lengths to get his attention; this must be a dream. "Why would you think that? Unless of course you aren't interested?"

"I'd love to go out with you, but…"

"But what?"

"The woman…the one I saw you with in the store. From the looks of things, she wasn't just a regular customer."

"Oh, her." He laughed. "That was my sister, Susan."

Tension melted from Carolyn's shoulders. "Your sister? What a relief. I was afraid you and she…"

"Say no more. I get the picture. So, how about a date?"

"Like I said, I'd love to."

"That's great.   Are you busy tomorrow night? Perhaps dinner and a movie?"

"I'm free, and I can't think of anyone I'd rather share popcorn with." Her mouth hurt from such a broad smile.

"If you give me directions to your house, I'll pick you up at seven."

"Seven it is. I can't wait." She gave him street-by-street instructions and hung up. Turning, she noticed the grocery bags she'd left on the counter. Thank goodness nothing in them needed refrigeration. She turned her attention to putting away her earlier purchases, humming all the while.

* * * *

Carolyn stood at the bathroom sink and plucked at her hair, lifting the low spot at the crown. The reflection of her dark eyes sparkled with joy. She finally had a date. With so much time passed since the last one, she hoped she hadn't forgotten how to act.

She dabbed her favorite jasmine perfume behind each ear and at the pulsing spot just above her necklace. A glance over her shoulder at the full-length mirror showed no stray hair or lint. Her black pantsuit made her look pounds lighter, and she struck a voguish pose.

Her wristwatch showed only fifteen minutes before Mike was due to arrive. Her heartbeat quickened, and her mouth turned dry. She took a long breath and released it slowly, vowing to be herself.

She was just straightening up the bathroom when the doorbell rang. Making her way to the living room, her stomach flip-flopped, and an onset of nerves filled her head with doubts. Despite her trembling, she opened the door to find him standing on the porch. She caught a familiar whiff of his aftershave and smiled. If she had any doubts, it was too late now. "Won't you come in?" She made a sweeping gesture.

His gaze raked her from head to foot as he stepped inside. "You look lovely."

"Thank you." She dipped her chin, feeling her cheeks heat. How long had it been since she heard those words? She raised her head and assessed his gray slacks, pale blue shirt, and charcoal blazer. "You look quite handsome yourself."

Panic seized her and flooded her mind with warnings. God, she'd let him into her house without a second thought. What did she really know about this man? Her insides churned like a mixer. Did she look green yet?

She swallowed hard and took a breath. He had the eyes and demeanor of a decent man, and she'd always been a good judge of character. Surely, he was what he appeared to be. Who could blame her if she wanted a "stop and smell the roses" moment. At her age, not many years remained to live it up.

"Are you set to go?" He pulled her from her thoughts and motioned to the door.

"Yes, let me grab my purse, and we'll be off."

He stood behind her as she locked the house then escorted her to his king cab pickup. After opening the door, he held her hand as she stepped up on the running board and slid onto the seat. "That's a big leap for such a petite lady."

Her nerves jangled. If he only knew how big a leap she'd made. What if he was a con-man or worse, a serial killer? Now was a fine time to conjure up all the bad things that might happen. If worse came to worse, Sally knew who to finger when the authorities found Carolyn's dead body. She released a pent-up breath and tried to relax. Thankfully, soft music drifted from the radio, making the silence not nearly so awkward.

* * * *

Dinner was delicious, the talk smooth and easy, and the movie romantic and over way too soon. At one point, he'd reached over and grasped her hand. The connection felt natural. Time passed too quickly, but on the drive home, they shared more talk of family, friends, and finances, and enjoyed the comfort of feeling nothing was too sacred to discuss. If he'd been a priest, her confessions couldn't have been more personal. It all felt right. When Mike said he'd love to see her again, her mind played pictures of all the things they might do in the future: a cruise, an overnight camping trip in the RV he mentioned he had, a trip to an amusement park to justify the lost childish feelings he'd brought back to her.

At her house, like the perfect gentleman, he walked around, opened her door, and helped her out of the vehicle. Accompanying her to the door, he held her hand. The dampness between their palms displayed both were nervous about ending the date. Carolyn tugged her hand free and fished for her keys. When she unlocked the door, again her mouth turned to cotton, and she hoped this wasn't their last date—hoped he hadn't just said what she wanted to hear.

Turning to him, she looked up and smiled. "I had a wonderful time."

The porch light reflected in his blue eyes. "I did, too. Would it be too presumptuous of me to ask you out again tomorrow night?"

His question stole the breath from her lungs. Her heart soared. "Not at all. I'd love it."

A small gasp escaped her when he bent and kissed her—his lips soft against hers. When she didn't pull away, he gathered her in his arms and gazed down at her with a smile. "As we say in the shoe business, this feels like just the perfect fit."

The End

Masked Love

"You want me to what?" Olivia Wilson stared at Doctor Ray. The paper on the examining table crinkled with her shocked movement.

"A lot of people wear one and eventually get used to it."

"But what if I don't want to?" She eyed the contraption he dangled in the air that looked like something he'd snatched from a scuba diver.

"If you'll recall, when you agreed to the overnight study, we discussed sleep apnea which I suspected causes your constant fatigue, and the tests prove me right. People who suffer from the disorder often stop breathing for ten seconds or longer during sleep. The problem can be mild to severe, based on the number of times each hour you fail to take a breath or how often your lungs don't get enough air. This may happen from five to fifty times an hour and can be fatal. Your results fall within these parameters."

"You mean I could die?" She swallowed hard.

"Possibly, unless you use the CPAP machine and wear this mask." He extended his arm.

"Here, try it on."

Olivia rolled her eyes. "Oh please, say it isn't so. Aren't I suffering enough by battling a weight problem and facing middle age? Now you want me to don something that makes me look alien."

He chuckled. "I'm not asking you to wear it twenty-four hours a day—only at night."

"Great!" She clenched her teeth. "I'm forty-two, single, trying to find a man without any

help from Victoria's Secret because nothing she makes fits me, and now I'm supposed to wear a snorkel at night and be connected to a little machine that blows air up my nose. Grand, just grand."

Doctor Ray grasped her shoulder. "Livie, I've known you most of your life. I wouldn't suggest something unless I really believe you need it. As long as you carry that extra fifty pounds around, you're going to have to use this machine every night, and that's a fact."

Despite the archaic colors on the walls and floor tile and the outdated equipment, her implicit faith in Doctor Ray hadn't dimmed. After all, she'd been coming here for years. Regardless, her eyes welled with tears, and she blew a blast of air upward to dry them. Clearing her throat, she tried to find a calm voice. "I trust you, but what man wants a woman who looks like Jacques Cousteau?"

He covered his mouth to hide his smile then slid his hand down and grasped his white goatee. "Maybe this mask will be the kick in the behind you need to lose the weight you gained since you and Denny divorced. Like so many unhappy people, you turned to food for comfort. If you hate using the equipment enough, perhaps you'll find something to occupy your time besides eating."

The doc's words sliced through her like a knife. The truth always hurt. Olivia never expected Denny to leave her after seventeen years, and for another woman, but he had. He'd been gone for two years, and all the snacking she'd done at night had brought her to this moment. God, she hated herself. Why couldn't she hate Denny? After all those years of cooking, cleaning, doing his laundry, and having sex whenever he wanted, he'd left her for a younger woman. What a bastard.

Livie dipped her chin and stared at the floor. "I always laughed when I watched movies where the hero said, 'I love you, but I'm not in love with you,' because the line sounded so stupid. Guess what, the phrase isn't nearly as funny when you hear it from your husband." She gazed up through blurry eyes. "How can I fall out of love? I still miss him."

Doctor Ray shook his head. "I can tend fractured limbs and other ailments, but I have no fix for a broken heart." He patted the back of her hand. "You and time are the only two things that can heal that pain, but I'll gladly suggest a great nutritionist who'll help you with your diet."

He crossed the room and sat on his rolling stool. "Say the word and I'll give you a referral."

Olivia massaged her brow. Her back was against the proverbial wall, but maybe this was what she needed to jumpstart her life again. Denny had remarried a year ago and probably never gave her a thought. She needed to move on and find someone new or resolve herself to living alone. If healing meant wearing a mask at night until she lost the extra pounds, then….

Straightening her shoulders, she managed a smile. "Okay, sign me up. I've wasted enough of my life."

"First, you'll need to pick up a CPAP machine from the medical supply house on Fifteenth Street. I've already faxed your information, and they'll have the settings appropriate for your needs. They'll also be your maintenance and supply contact." He handed her a yellow slip and a prescription form. "You'll need these to get the machine." He scribbled out another note on his RX pad. "And here's the referral to Dr. Tricia Yates. She's very well known in the field of nutrition, and I'm sure the doc can get you on a daily regime you can follow easily. Once you lose the weight, you'll probably discover you won't need the machine for sleep apnea any longer."

"Well I suppose there's some good news hidden in there somewhere." Olivia slid from the table and crossed to where her purse sat on a chair. She tucked the referral in a side pocket and slung the shoulder bag in place. "Thank you, Dr. Ray, for everything. I promise the next time you see me, there won't be quite so much to view." Olivia's laughter sounded forced, even to her.

"Good luck to you, dear, and if any more questions come up, please call my office."

* * * *

Olivia clutched the top of her purse in a fisted hand and opened the door to the medical supply house. Already her cheeks burned like she'd been in the sun too long, and she hadn't even faced the clerk yet. At seeing the counter vacant, she considered turning around, getting back in her car, and forgetting the whole ordeal, but doing that wouldn't solve her problem. The word "death" kept ringing in her ears. Was pride more important than life? Sometimes she wondered, especially with her own existence so empty and sad.

Her hand hovered over the silver bell with a note that said, "ring for service." Olivia took a deep breath, depressed the plunger, and grimaced at the annoying tinkle. Too late to turn back now, she squared her shoulders.

The curtains behind the counter parted, and her

breath hitched at the handsome man who strode through them. "Hello, may I help you?"

Dark hair, blue eyes, broad shoulders, a little extra weight, but still a piece of eye candy. Her fleeting scan of him didn't miss a thing. Latching onto the counter's edge, she steadied her weak knees. "Y-yes…I…I…" Words failed her, and she shoved the wrinkled papers toward him.

He smoothed out the crumpled sheets. "Ah, so you're Olivia. I'm Austin Reed, and I received Dr. Ray's fax. I have everything ready for you."

She dipped her chin. "This is rather embarrassing."

"You shouldn't feel that way." The clerk's tone was sympathetic. "This is a medical situation and nothing to beat yourself up over. This store services more people in the community than you can imagine."

She looked up and smiled. "I never thought I'd be one of those people. In fact, I had no idea I had sleep apnea."

"Most people don't, but I'm sure you'll feel a difference once you start sleeping with the mask on."

She gave a shuddering head-shake. "That's what creeps me out."

"The mask? It's really not that horrible, but ladies usually have vanity issues about wearing one. Is that what's bothering you, or are you really afraid?" He tilted his head.

"A little of both, I think."

"A pretty lady like you shouldn't worry yourself over sleeping in something that will help you breathe better. Let me get your equipment and explain how to use it." He disappeared between the curtains.

Had he just called her a pretty lady? Of course he had. He was a salesman, after all. No one with his good looks would be interested in her any further than the monthly fee she had to pay him to look ridiculous. Her mouth turned dryer than the Sahara, and she fished in her bag for a piece of gum.

Austin returned with a small box and set it on the counter. "The machine isn't very big, and we provide you with lots of tubing so you can roll over without yanking everything off onto the floor."

As he pulled the contents out one-by-one, she eyed each piece with disdain, while sneaking the gum into her mouth then stuffing the wrapper in her pocket. The sweet taste of strawberries summoned back her saliva. If there was a bright spot to this whole apnea thing, maybe it would be rolling over one night and strangling herself to death with the length of flexible plastic hose.

"This," he held up the mask, "is what fits over your face and feeds air up your nose, so you are always getting enough oxygen. I've plugged in the settings from your sleep study, so you can start using it tonight."

"What about the machine?" She curled her upper lip at the digitalized contraption.

"All you need to do is turn it off and on. Everything is programmed. We'll recheck the calibrations on occasion to make sure the settings remain appropriate for your needs, and you'll be eligible for new tubing and mask every few months." He pulled a folder from beneath the box and thumbed through the pages. "It looks like your insurance will cover all the associated costs except for the minimal replacement charges for the mask and tubing." He glanced up. "Do you have any questions for me?"

His blue eyes sparkled more than the diamond ring she used to wear on her left hand. A quick scan showed he wore no adornment on his finger either. And questions....

What are you doing the rest of your life, popped into her mind, but a red flag waved through her thoughts—he might be one of those men who didn't wear a wedding band.

Olivia simply shook her head. "I think I understand everything you've explained, and it looks like the instruction booklet will help if anything strange crops up."

He put the contents back inside the box. "Please feel free to call anytime you need my help."

With the tubing coiled atop the machine, he sealed the carton with tape then took a business card from a plastic stand and handed it to her. "The second number listed here is for emergencies. You'll reach an answering service that will contact me right away."

She accepted the card and put it in her purse. "Thank you, you've been most helpful."

"Let me carry this out to your car for you." He tucked the carton under his arm and stepped around the counter.

He opened the door, rattling the venetian blinds, and followed her outside. "Lovely weather, isn't it?"

She peered up at the fluffy, white clouds floating in the sea of blue, and nodded. "Perfect for doing some gardening. Since I live alone, everything falls on my shoulders."

Now that life circumstances forced her to wear a snorkel at night, she'd probably live alone forever. Heaving a sigh, she clicked her remote control and unlocked the doors of her car. While he placed the box on the passenger seat, she slid behind the wheel. The sweet aroma of his aftershave wafted over and tickled her nose. She inhaled deeply and smiled. He smelled as wonderful as he looked.

Realizing he stared at her, she grasped the wheel

with one hand and fumbled to fit the key into the ignition with the other. What the hell was wrong with her? The man probably thought her a fool. She certainly felt like one. Her high school years were long gone, yet she acted exactly like she had eons ago when a boy gave her tummy butterflies. Austin Reed had just unleashed a whole swarm of them in her belly, and he didn't have a clue.

Anxious to retreat from the awkward moment she created, Olivia cleared her throat and turned to him. "Thank you again for your help, Mr. Reed."

"Austin, please." He withdrew from bending over the seat, yet crouched low enough for her to see his face. "It's been my pleasure, and do call me if you need anything at all."

He no sooner closed the door than she backed out of the parking space. Perhaps a little faster than intended as bits of gravel pelted the car's underside. Call if she needed anything? He'd certainly be shocked if he knew what ran through her mind. God, she'd been without a man for too long.

* * * *

At home, Olivia opened the closet and stashed the box on the shelf. Mixed emotions tied her insides in a knot. On one hand, not using the machine tested fate and her health, but on the other, she had no desire to look like a freak. Denny's leaving created an aura of self-doubt and insecurity that hung over her head like a dark cloud. Who in the world would want to sleep in the same bed with someone akin to the elephant man? And why was she considering another man in the first place. Stood to reason she'd have to find a willing soul before she could charm him into her bed.

The only guy she'd ever loved had broken her heart. Regardless, she just couldn't face making her decision about the CPAP right now.

Never more than a social drinker, she craved something to numb her pain. Olivia couldn't blame Denny for her apnea problem, but he was at fault for the rest of her hang-ups.

Holding the remote, she curled into a ball on the sofa and flipped on the TV. Just her luck, the SciFi channel featured a special on deep-sea diving. Tears she'd fought all day, streamed down her cheeks.

* * * *

Fear won out. Earlier in the morning Olivia woke, gasping for air. Still being stubborn, she had huffed into a paper bag for ten minutes before she'd accepted reality. Breathing meant living, and she wasn't ready to give up on life yet.

She'd approached the closet several times during the day, but now at bedtime, she put her vanity aside, faced the inevitable, and took down the box holding the CPAP machine.

Clad in the cartoon character pajamas she'd received as a last gift from Denny, and certainly befitting the occasion, Olivia balanced on the edge of her mattress and fingered the headgear attached to her new mask.

She released a loud whoosh of air and prepared to dress for battle. Maybe if she pretended she was fighting germ warfare, the whole idea might not seem quite so bad. She tossed the snorkel-looking device onto the bed and lowered her face into her open palms.

Who was she fooling? Tears welled in her eyes, and a lump formed in her throat. The last few years of her life had been nothing but challenges, mostly unpleasant ones, and her current dilemma rated second worst on the list—right after divorce. Maybe she could do one more night mask-free. If death claimed her, would anyone really miss her? She'd given Denny everything and he hadn't even left her with a child. With her mother and father gone, she had absolutely no one with whom she felt close.

After a good cry drained all her tears, she resolved to follow Dr. Ray's orders. She'd depended on a husband to make her decisions for too many years. The time had come to take back her life.

Tomorrow, she'd call the nutritionist, get on a more healthy regime, and like the doctor said, possibly eliminate the need for the apnea gadget. Before Olivia talked herself out of it, she slipped the rubber banding over her head and adjusted the nose-piece to fit her face. With a press of a button, a gentle stream of air filtered through the tubing and up her nostrils. After turning out the light, she stretched out on the bed, closed her eyes, and pretended she was on a beach where a cooling breeze washed over her—especially her face. Sometime during her faux tour to Tahiti, she drifted off to sleep.

* * * *

Olivia pushed aside her unopened mail—mostly bills, and checked the calendar on her desk. Three weeks had passed since she'd gotten her CPAP machine, and she hadn't missed a single night using it. She'd always been a sucker when it came to suggestion, but in all honesty she felt more rested upon waking in the mornings.

Her first meeting with her nutritionist had gone well, and for the past two weeks, Olivia had avoided chips, chocolate, and soda—her three prior dietary mainstays. Steering clear of the extra calories came a little easier when reminding herself that losing weight would help rid her of the little machine sitting on her nightstand.

What she needed was a job, even though the divorce settlement awarded her the house and her car plus a tidy sum of monthly alimony. Denny had insisted she be 'Suzy Homemaker.'

Cleaning house, paying bills, picking up dry-cleaning, tending to his every need had been her responsibility for years. Their plans to have children never materialized because her monthly cycles were so irregular, at least that was the reason given by her OB/GYN doctor, but she believed for the last couple of years, Denny had cheated on her and wasn't interested in sex at home. Before then, she often wondered if Denny had gotten a vasectomy and didn't tell her. Olivia wouldn't put it past him because he never really seemed interested in children and always changed the subject when the topic of starting a family arose. Livie really wanted a baby, and the tick of her biological clock was so loud, she heard it. Denny had been a controlling jerk, and she allowed it. Why did it take her so long to figure that out?

A job! Despite any type of resume, she'd make that a priority. If she got out of the house more often, maybe she'd meet someone. Her daily walks around the neighborhood as part of her weight loss strategy only garnered waves from old Mr. Higgins who lived on the corner and sat on his front porch in a wicker rocking chair most of the day. He had to be eighty by now.

As she tied the laces on her walking shoes, the phone rang. She crossed to the desk and answered.

"Hello, is this Olivia?" The voice sounded somewhat familiar.

"Yes. Who's this?"

"Austin Reed from the Mountain Medical Supply."

Her breath caught in her throat.

"I'm calling to see how things are working out with your machine."

She swallowed hard, picturing those sky blue eyes and broad shoulders. "F-fine. I don't much care for the darn thing, but I am using it every night."

"That's good to hear."

A long pause ensued.

"Are you still there?" she asked.

"Ah…yes. I admit I hoped you might be having some sort of difficulty requiring my services, but since you seem to have everything under control, I'll man up and come to the point."

Her interest piqued. Had her insurance failed to pay him? How embarrassing! She nibbled her bottom lip.

"I would very much like to ask you to dinner, Olivia. I know you barely know me, but unless we go out, I have no idea how we'll become better acquainted."

Stunned into speechlessness, her mouth dropped open. She pinched her forearm to make sure she really was awake. Austin Reed phoned to ask her out?

"Are you still there?" Now he asked.

Glad he couldn't see her broad smile, she gulped back a chuckle. "Y-yes, I'm here. Just a little stunned."

"I know, I know," he sounded flustered. "I'm being very presumptuous, but I kept remembering the little detail you dropped about being on your own and fought calling you. I've been divorced for a number of years, dated a few times, but when nothing worked out between me and lady friends, I started burying myself in my work to forget how lonely I really am. I'd love if you'd accept my invitation to dine with me tomorrow night."

"I'd love to." The words tumbled out before she gave his offer a second thought. Her cheeks flushed warm with excitement.

"Great! I have your address. Do you have a food and time preference?"

"I'm sure anything you pick will be fine with me." Anything, and she meant it. If he made mud patties and served them up, she'd eat them just to spend time with him. She held the phone away from her face. Okay, well maybe not mud patties. She grimaced and smacked her lips at the taste the thought conjured up before putting the phone back to her mouth. "Ah, I can be ready at seven. Is that okay?"

"Seven works for me. I'll be on your doorstep then. See you tomorrow evening."

Olivia hung up and clutched the phone to her bosom. A date? She hadn't had one for years—none since Denny. What would she wear? How would she style her hair? Her knees turned weak, and she side-stepped to the sofa and sagged down on the floral cushion. Her friend and neighbor, Cora, would never believe it.

Feeling more composed, Olivia dialed Cora's number.

"Hello."

"Cora, you won't believe this, I know you won't. You'd better sit down. Remember the handsome man I told you about at the medical supply…you know the one with blue eyes and shoulders to die for? Well—"

"Hold on, Livie. Lord, take a breath. You're making me tired just listening to your prattle. Now, slow and easy, tell me your news."

Good ol' Cora. Always calm, cool, collected, and the person Olivia always counted on for support. Without her, Olivia might have done something rash when Denny left.

Olivia took a breath. "Sorry, I'm just so excited."

"I think I could tell." Cora chuckled.

"Austin just called and asked me out to dinner. Tomorrow at seven."

"And, of course, you accepted."

"Why wouldn't I? The man is dreamy."

"Usually, I would tell you to be careful because you don't know him at all, but since he's a local businessman, and I have friends who interact with him, I wish you a wonderful evening."

"What if I make a bad impression? What should I do? What should I talk about? Are there things I should avoid?"

"Calm down, Olivia. Remember who you're asking. I haven't been on a date in ages. Larry stopped asking me out about twenty-five years ago. I guess my advice is just be yourself.   Let the conversation come naturally, and if something feels comfortable to discuss, then talk about whatever comes to mind."

"Will you come over tomorrow and help me choose what to wear? Oh, I wish I had started my diet sooner. I look so fat in everything I own."

"Didn't you meet him before you even made your first appointment with the nutritionist?"

"Yes, but…"

"No buts. He must have liked what he saw if he called and asked you out."

"Do you think so?"

"I think the facts speak for themselves. Now I've got to go and get Larry's dinner on the table or I'll hear about it when he comes home from golfing. Call me tomorrow when you're ready to go through your closet."

"Okay and thanks." Olivia put the phone back on its cradle and stared into space. Her life had become so boring, what could she possibly find to discuss that would be of interest to Austin?

* * * *

The drive was painlessly short, and Olivia widened her eyes at the plush interior when they walked into Victorio's Restaurant. She'd often driven by but never expected to be a patron. The maitre'd seated them at the table Austin had reserved and left them holding elegant leather menus with the establishment's name etched in gold.

"Wow, this place is beautiful," she leaned forward in the red velvet booth and whispered.

"I hoped you'd approve of my choice." He opened his menu and stared into it.

"Who wouldn't want to have dinner in a place this lovely?" She opened her own bill of fare and gulped at the prices. What if she ordered something too expensive? Nothing listed was less than twenty-five dollars. The few times Denny took her out to dinner, their combined bill didn't reach that amount.

"How about we start with some champagne?"

Her gaze caught the cost of one bottle, and she tried not to gasp. "Whatever you think is fine with me."

Austin motioned to the waiter, asked for a bottle of their best, and then turned his gaze on her. "Did I tell you how lovely you look tonight?"

Her cheeks warm, she stared into her lap and smoothed the dress she'd chosen for the occasion. Nothing said slim like black. "Thank you. A woman never tires of hearing praise like that."

"Would you like an appetizer?"

Would she! Yes, but what she wanted wasn't on the menu. She fisted her hands at her inappropriate thoughts, but his lips were too tempting not to notice. She gazed at him and smiled. "I'm fine without anything before dinner. I'm actually trying to lose some weight."

"I think you look great just as you are, but I know what it's like to try to shed a few pounds. I battle temptation all the time."

"Really." She tilted her head. "I think you look very dashing in your suit."

Had she really said *dashing?* What next…slaying a dragon, or asking where he'd left the white stallion he rode in on to save her from her lonely existence? She knew her face was beet red—she felt it. Maybe he'd attribute the scarlet tinge to a reflection from the upholstery. She bit her tongue to silence her stupidity, but thankfully, the waiter brought the champagne and saved her from more embarrassing rhetoric.

He poured the amber liquid into their glasses,

handed them over, then departed.

Olivia took the half-filled flute and sipped. The bubbles tickled her nose, and the sweet taste lingered on her tongue. One taste led to another, and before she realized her thirst, she'd drained her glass. Austin reached across the table and poured a refill. "Would you like to order now?"

She stared at the open menu on the table. "What do you suggest?" Asking seemed the safest way to make her dinner selection.

"How about the lobster for two?"

Seafood had never been her favorite, but she'd asked his opinion. She feigned a smile.

"Sounds wonderful."

* * * *

Olivia set the candelabra on the table and placed the slim white tapers in their holders.
Tonight would be her fifth date with Austin. They'd been out to eat twice, gone to the movies, bowled, and took a ride out in the country and parked next to a lake. His kisses were just as awesome as she'd imagined, and he stirred passions she'd thought long dead. Gentleman that he was, he never made an improper move. Should she be flattered or worry? Perhaps tonight would put her question to rest.

After dinner, she planned for the two of them to enjoy her favorite movie, Ghost, on her VCR. She'd amassed quite a collection of tapes that now seemed only good as long as her machine lasted. DVDs, Blue Ray, and live streaming direct to one's computer were all the rage, but she just couldn't see spending money on new media when her old equipment still worked perfectly fine.

Olivia moved the movie to the top of the stack, turned on the stereo, another defunct item, this one playing cassettes instead of CDs, then selected a collection of easy listening music she'd taped for her own listening pleasure.

With everything ready in the dining room, she scurried into the kitchen to check the stuffed pork chops in the oven. The salad was made, the baked beans simmering; everything was ready, except her. She set the oven to warm and hurried to the bedroom.

Olivia glanced at her reflection in the dresser mirror. Her shoulder-length brown hair hung in damp ringlets around her face, and her white blouse bore splatter stains from dumping the can contents into a bowl. She'd spent so much time making sure everything was dusted and clean, she'd lost track of time. After checking the clock, she grabbed a clean towel from the linen closet and made a beeline for the bathroom. While waiting for the water to warm, she pictured herself in the new outfit she'd bought to celebrate losing her first ten pounds. The cleavage-exposing top and snug jeans were sure to draw Austin's attention. She already felt more attractive…and sexy.

* * * *

Dinner over, the candles had burned to the halfway mark. Their flames flickered in shadows on the walls, and the three glasses of wine Olivia had savored made the room overly warm.

Austin's shoulders looked extremely broad in his blue polo shirt, and the sexy music playing in the background made her want to be in his arms—taste his kisses again.

As if reading her mind, he came and stood next to her chair. "May I have this dance?"

"Of course." She took his offered hand, rose, and then lacking balance from over-imbibing, sagged against him. "Sorry, I'm a bit tipsy. I think I should have stopped at two glasses of wine." She snickered.

"Some people would consider you a cheap drunk." He peered down and winked as he tightened his arm around her waist and reeled her closer.

She rested her head against his shoulder and swayed to the tempo of 'Three Times a Lady'.

The song had always been a favorite, and she hummed along. Moved by the lyrics, she pressed her body against his, allowing her alcohol-induced state to provide blinders to her boldness. She lifted her chin and smiled. Blessed was the day Doc Ray had sent her to the medical supply for that damned CPAP machine. Austin was living proof that good things often came from bad.

His face blurred when he bent and claimed her mouth. She closed her eyes, languishing in the warmth seeping into her nether region. So much time had passed since she'd felt like a woman. Her lips parted to his probing tongue.

The kiss deepened. Passion tingled her toes and ignited a flame that climbed upward. The sexual needs she'd denied for so long screamed to be satisfied. Did she dare push aside her fears and plunge headlong into the most intimate of all acts? Her heart ruled her brain…or the wine did.

Olivia stepped out of his embrace but kept hold of his hand. With a nod of her head toward the bedroom, she led the way. He followed without a word. Once they were in the confines of her boudoir, and she'd turned on a small lamp, she stepped back into his arms. The hunger in her kiss transmitted her need for more, and he responded by grinding his hardness against her. Still entwined in one another's arms, they inched toward the bed and collapsed onto it. Words weren't needed as their fingers clawed at buttons and snaps. She kicked off her jeans while Austin stood, pulled his shirt over his head, shed his shoes, and dropped his trousers.

On the bed, clad only in her panties, she eyed the furry mat on his chest with appreciation, especially the thin trail leading to the waistband of his bulging boxer shorts. He removed his underwear and joined her on the bed. She tried not to admire his manhood openly, but found it difficult to draw her gaze away. She turned off the light and rolled to face him. Somewhere in the middle of caresses and kisses, she lost her hip-hugging briefs and any reservations she had about intimacy with Austin.

In the aftermath of lovemaking, they lay side by side on their backs, waiting for their respirations to slow. Her perfume and his aftershave mingled together with the earthy smell of recent sex. Olivia rested her head on his shoulder. "You're a wonderful lover," she whispered.

He turned his head and grinned. "I was just thinking the same about you."

Her wine haze gone, the reality of what had happened slapped her hard. She raised her head from his shoulder and peered into his eyes. "You don't think me forward do you?"

"Not at all, Livie, We're adults, after all."

She warmed at his tone, and he'd called her Livie. No one except Dr. Ray and those who'd known her since childhood used that name. She splayed her fingers through Austin's chest hair. "I know we're of consenting age, but I never knew I could be so bold."

"Well, I like when you are, so don't stop." He leaned over and bussed her lips.

Tiredness tugged at her eyelids, and her body sagged with the relaxation that only came after sex. "Will you spend the night with me?" She cuddled closer.

"A-ah, I'd love to, but I can't."

She wanted to ask why but didn't really want to know the answer. Had she disappointed him? He appeared satisfied, but maybe she didn't compare to others he'd been with. Her contentment sunk like a stone in the pit of her belly.

Austin rolled off the bed and disappeared into the bathroom, leaving her to ponder her misgivings. When he returned, she rolled to the bed's opposite side while he dressed. She couldn't bear to watch him leave.

Her previous sense of relaxation gone, she questioned her worth again. Had she given herself up too soon and to the wrong person? Tears welled in her eyes and she struggled against crying. The last thing she wanted was his pity.

His warm hand rested on her arm. "No need to get up. I'll see myself out and lock the door behind me." He stretched across the bed and kissed her cheek. "Thank you for a wonderful evening."

Words failed her. One minute they shared each other with such pleasure, and now he was leaving. She tugged the blanket higher to hide her tears, but set free her pent up sobs the moment she heard the front door close.

* * * *

The phone ringing on her nightstand woke her. She slapped around in the darkness until she found it then struggled to get it past the plastic tubing of her CPAP. "Hullo." She answered in a sleepy haze, mumbling through her mask.

"Livie, I'm sorry for calling so late, but I've been thinking…" Austin's voice yanked her into wakefulness.

She pushed up on one elbow, switched off her machine and tugged off her snorkel. "Thinking about what?"

"How much I wanted to spend the night with you—to wake up next to you in the morning."

"Then why didn't you?" There, she'd asked the question she dreaded.

"Promise not to laugh?"

She sagged back on her pillow, the phone pressed to her ear and apprehension tweaking her muscles. "I promise."

"I-I…"

"You can tell me." She insisted. "I can take it." She grimaced at her feigned bravery. Could she really handle what he had to say?

"I adored making love to you. You're such a wonderful woman, and I bless the day we met, but…"

His beating around the proverbial bush was agony. "What is it, Austin. You're killing me here."

"I-I had to come home, because I didn't bring my CPAP machine with me. I didn't expect you to invite me to stay."

The tenseness melted away like candlewax in the sunlight. That was it? He wore a CPAP at night, too.

Although she promised not to laugh, a giggle of relief bubbled up. She swallowed it. "Oh, Austin, I thought it was something much more serious. Although I admit I worried over whether or not to forgo using my mask for the night if you had stayed."

"I hope you understand. I have to use mine. If I don't, I snore like a freight train, and I'm one of those who really stops breathing without the aid of my machine."

"I certainly understand. Using mine has made a huge difference in my life, too, but promise me something, will you?"

"Of course, anything."

"Next time you come for dinner or a visit, bring your apparatus with you."

"Is tomorrow night too soon?"

"I look forward to it." She smacked her lips in a loud kiss goodnight and hung up the phone.

She replaced her mask, turned on her machine and snuggled down beneath the covers, finally releasing the giggle she earlier denied. She'd read a hundred romance novels where the hero wore something to disguise his face, but she never imagined her lover would sport a mask, too. With a soft sigh, she drifted to sleep, visions of the Lone Ranger in her head.

The End

Masked Love

Hurricane Warning

"Batten down the hatches, folks." The radio weatherman's half-hearted chuckle did little to lighten the mood. His earlier forecast about an approaching storm proved true.

Linda Morrison peered through the picture window of her new Florida home and watched the whitecaps churning in Sleepy Reef's inlet. Although the word 'hurricane' had yet to be uttered, the sky grew darker by the minute and rain fell in torrents. Raging wind carried the spray from the crashing tide high into the air and whipped the colored flags atop the boathouse into a frantic dance. She chewed her bottom lip.

A few months ago, she'd lived in the Midwest and feared tornadoes. Moving here had simply switched one of Mother Nature's furies for another. Why hadn't Linda considered that possibility?

She backed away from the shimmying window. If things worsened, she'd have to cover the glass panes to keep them from shattering, but she wasn't sure she could do it alone.

This was supposed to be her new start, not a nightmare. She'd purchased the home from an older couple who wanted to move closer to their children. The real estate agent had laughed when Linda asked what the sheets of plywood in the garage were used for. After Katrina, the woman found it hard to believe anyone wasn't versed in hurricane history.

Linda wrung her hands. She'd seen pictures of the aftermath of those violent winds and raging water…even felt sorrow for those who lived in the area, but right now, her main concern was whether or not her new property investment was about to be blown into a pile of sticks. She stepped to the television, switched it on, and searched for a more detailed weather report.

On a local channel, a sandy-haired man with a pointed nose stood in front of an area map. At once, the image faded to a pinpoint circle then went completely black as the power failed.

Linda's pulse quickened. Night hadn't yet fallen, but the storm's gray overcast masked the sun and made it seem much later than three in the afternoon.

"Oh, God. I haven't a clue where I put storm supplies when I unpacked." She searched her memory for the place she'd stashed the candles then pawed through the nearby drawers in the dining room hutch. She found two tapers wedged beneath her linen napkins. Although they weren't what she sought, they'd work. She'd barely placed them in the silver candelabra on the dining room table when someone knocked. Putting match to wick, a flame sputtered to life and danced in silhouettes on the wall. She flicked her wrist to extinguish the burning wood that shrunk dangerously close to her fingertips. A second knock sounded.

"Who in the world would be out in this weather?" she mumbled. On her way to find out, she stubbed her toe on the leg of the coffee table and groaned. The pain intense, she stumbled on to the foyer.

When she turned the doorknob, the wind's force caught the door and heaved it inward. The blast blew her off balance, but she steadied herself and used her weight to keep the oak portal partially closed to the blowing rain. Someone in a yellow parka huddled on her doorstep.

"May I help you?" Linda asked, whisking a wayward hair away from her mouth, her tone unwelcoming.

A face materialized from beneath the slicker. Masculine eyes, dark as onyx peered at her. "I was wondering the same."

He swept back his hood, allowing his ebony hair to dance in the blustery current. His square jaw and tanned face softened with a smile. "I'm your neighbor from down the street. I thought perhaps you might need some assistance. My sister, Marcie, tells me you live alone. If this storm notches itself up a bit, we're in for a turbulent night."

Against warning bells about strangers, she sought escape from the elements. She knew his sister…maybe, the name rang vaguely familiar. "Please, come in." Linda gestured, but kept a tight grip on the door to keep it from slamming into the wall. Her heart thudded. Would her murder top the evening news? She could just see the headline now, "Stupid woman opens door to stranger during storm."

He stopped on the throw rug just inside and wiped his feet. Water ran in rivulets from his plastic coat, rather defeating his purpose. His wet hair drooped on a smooth forehead and gave him a boyish appearance. "My name is Carlos Mejia. You met my sister when she came and delivered her 'welcome to the neighborhood' casserole."

Sweet relief. Her pulse slowed. He wasn't a complete stranger, per se.

"Oh, of course, Marcie. We had a very nice visit. She told me she lived with her brother, but for some reason I pictured a much younger one." Linda chuckled, but her cheeks heated. Carlos was definitely not a child. The shoulders beneath his slicker stretched almost as wide as the doorway. She hadn't seen anyone so handsome in a long time.

Her gaze drifted to her attire and her nose twitched. If only she'd put on something more impressive than her oldest jeans and a faded tee shirt.

"Do you mind if I take off this wet coat?" His deep voice summoned her attention.

"How rude of me. Of course not, please, let me have that drippy thing, and I'll hang it somewhere to dry."

Shadows deepened.

"Seems we've lost our candlelight to the wind." She crossed to the table and struck a flame to the blackened wicks.

Linda turned back to him and her breath hitched. Carlos wore a tank top, baring biceps she'd only seen on weight lifters. A tattoo of barbed wire circled his left arm, complete with two bright crimson blood drops. It must have taken the artist an awful long time to circle all that muscle. She released a slow and steady breath.

Realizing she stared, she raised her gaze. "H-here, let me have your coat now."

"Thanks." His smile displayed a darling dimple. He handed over his wet garment then trailed behind her to the laundry room.

She draped his coat across the dryer and turned. "I'm..." They stood almost nose-to-nose.

Taking a step back and pressed against the washing machine, she flashed an awkward smile. "I'm glad to see you. I worried I wouldn't be able to cover the windows by myself if need be."

He crossed his arms, flexing his muscles and increasing the size of his biceps. "That's why I'm here. Do you have a battery-operated radio? We should listen to a forecast and find out the latest developments."

Linda tapped her chin. "Let me think. I believe it's in the bedroom closet. I hope the batteries are still good."

Carlos blocked the doorway and showed no intention of moving. Had she made a mistake being so trusting? She swallowed hard. "If you'll step aside, I'll go and get the radio. I think we'd be much more comfortable in the living room."

Her tight shoulders relaxed when he moved and made a slight bow. "Sorry, I didn't mean to get in the way. After you, ma'am."

"Thank you, sir." A silent breath escaped her pursed lips.

A glance over her shoulder, and she released a loud breath. He hadn't followed her.

Standing on tiptoes, she found the old portable AM/FM on a closet shelf and toted it back into the living room.

On the coffee table, the radio came to life when she turned the knob. Carlos took over and dialed in the weather station and then leaned back on the sofa.

"We've upgraded to a possible hurricane. Listeners are advised to take necessary precautions and stay tuned for updates as they become available." The announcer's voice issued the very information they sought.

Linda's mouth gaped. "Oh my, what does he mean exactly?"

"I take it you've never been in a bad storm." Carlos

looked amazingly calm.

"No, where I'm from they have thunderstorms and an occasional tornado warning, but I've never been in a hurricane. Have you?"

"A long time ago. We have threats often, but Sleepy Reef usually catches the tail end of the storms. You still have to take precautions, though. Just in case."

She fisted her nervous hands and sat straighter. "So, what do we do first?"

"Let's see, we have candles, a radio, and I'm assuming you have food. How about water

Have any in bottles?"

"Yes, two cases actually and plenty of canned goods. I'm sure there are more candles, and I believe I have fresh batteries for the radio, I just need to find where I've put them."

"How about a hammer and nails?"

"In the garage. When I became a single woman, I made a trip to the hardware store and bought the basics." She recalled feeling out of place, shopping in what she'd always considered 'male domain.' Beginning a collection of tools at the age of thirty-one may have appeared ridiculous to some, but she'd always had a man in her life to take care of those types of needs—and others.

She licked her lips. Carlos looked better by the minute. Those muscles, that smile…. She cleared her throat and mentally chastised herself for sexual thoughts when a hurricane loomed and she had much more urgent thing that needed tending.

"So what's first on the list?" If he only knew what she just imagined.

"Sounds like you have all the rations and supplies

you need. Let's brave the storm outside and get the windows covered."

The back door in the laundry room led to the garage. Linda grabbed her raincoat from the closet and led the way. She handed Carlos his slicker on the way out. "I'm not sure I'm up for this."

He smiled, exposing his alluring dimple again. "Don't worry. I'll do most of the work. You provide the moral support and nails."

"I think I can handle that." She flicked the garage light switch in futility and accidentally nudged a red metal can. A hint of gasoline wafted up to greet her. "I forgot about the power outage. There's a flashlight in the cabinet over there."

"Don't need it." Carlos inched past her Toyota and expertly released the electric garage door. He manually rolled it up, allowing daylight inside. "We'll need to get the plywood out this way."

A strong wind gust pushed Linda against the wall. She tottered backward then regained her balance. "Oh, my gosh. I've never felt such force before." She pulled her coat closed and fastened the buttons.

"I admit the wind has picked up since I left my house, but that little breeze is nothing compared to the real deal. We'd better hurry and get these boards up." He sidestepped back along the car to the boards leaning against the wall.

Linda walked over and grasped the end of one to help, but Carlos stood mid-sheet and picked the board up as if it weighed nothing at all and carried it away. "Well, okay then," she said, feeling useless.

"Bring the hammer and nails," he called back to her.

That she could do. She found them in her tool chest and followed him. The wind whipped her long hair into tangles and sent rain stinging into her eyes. She blinked and staggered against the gusts, but withstood the anguish of splinters long enough to help Carlos secure the wood in place and pass nails to him. The man was a savior.

* * * *

Linda sat on the couch and hugged herself against the chill. She'd lit more candles to compensate for the covered windows. Carlos knelt at the fireplace and held a match to the paper covering on her store-bought log. "I'm glad I picked up a few of those while shopping. I didn't really expect to need a roaring fire in Florida, but I like the ambiance sometimes."

The compressed wood caught fire and small flames flickered beyond the screen. Carlos came and sat next to her. "You're shivering." He tugged the afghan off the sofa's arm and wrapped it around her.

She snuggled down and pulled her legs up under the crocheted blanket. "I think it's more from fright than the cold. I can't imagine a stronger wind than what we just experienced."

Carlos rubbed his arms. "It is colder than normal. Bet you think I'm pretty silly for wearing something with no sleeves."

"I hadn't really thought about it." She lied. Like any woman in her right mind wouldn't admire those 'guns' and think about having them around her. She lapsed into mental images she ought not be having.

"It wasn't this chilly when I got dressed this

morning." His voice yanked her attention back to reality. "I was on my way to the gym."

"I'm glad you came by here on the way. I don't know what I would have done without you." She curled her knees under her body then adjusted her cover and focused her attention on him. "So tell me about yourself."

"Not much to tell. I spent some time in the army, trying to be all I could be, like they advertise, but it didn't work—don't much like taking orders. Got married and divorced...after discovering the woman I wed could out-bark any drill sergeant, and I'm living with my sis to help her out. Her husband passed away a couple of years back."

Linda dipped her chin. "I heard." She lifted her gaze. "It's one thing to be left alone, but with a child...."

"What about you?" Carlos swiveled sideways and rested in the vee where the sofa back and arm met.

"It's a boring story. I got married in my mid-twenties, but my husband wasn't content with only one woman in his life. I stayed with him, hoping maybe counseling would help, but it didn't. I asked him to leave, and he did with no regrets. Luckily, we didn't have children." She took a breath. "Then I decided I was bored with being an accountant and living in the middle of nowhere, so I sold the house and land awarded me in the divorce settlement, combined it with my savings and here I am."

"Why Florida?"

"I always dreamed of living close to the ocean, and when I saw this house on the Internet, I seized the opportunity to make my fantasy come true. I found a job with no problem, but I guess I should have researched the climate a little more. I never thought about hurricanes."

The wind outside whistled and groaned; an occasional surge emitted a high-pitch cry like a body in pain. Linda shifted her widening gaze from the door to the huge living room window. "I sure don't like the sound of this."

"I grew up here so I've gotten used to storms. Don't worry; I have a feeling this one is going to blow itself out before it gets here."

"I hope you're right." She sunk down further into the afghan.

His gaze wandered to the pictures on the mantle. "Who's the guy in the photo?"

"My brother, Andy. He's all I have in this world. My parents were killed in a car crash ten years ago." She sighed, still pained at the memory.

"I'm sorry." Carlos reached over and patted her shoulder.

His consoling caress sent warmth shooting down her arm and spreading through her chest. Although his work-roughened fingers snagged the yarn of her covering, his touch was gentle and caring. She subtly slid her afghan down and clasped her hands together to capture the spark he stirred. If only one could bottle that feeling.

"So where does your brother live?" Carlos broke the awkward silence.

"He's in Germany right now…Army. Guess he doesn't mind taking orders."

Carlos laughed. "Someone has to, I reckon. I've just never been very good at it. I don't mind being a partner, but…"

"What about your job? Are you the boss?"

"Yep. It's my own construction company. I make the rules."

"I'm impressed."

"Don't be. My business is small potatoes compared to what I aim to own one day. Right now, CM Builders consists of only me and five employees."

"Still, you're your own boss, and that says something." No longer cold, she dangled one foot to the floor and dropped her covering to her lap.

He leaned over to the coffee table. "Mind if I switch the station?"

"No, not at all." Had she embarrassed him? He dropped the topic so fast.

Voices blurred into a cacophony of sounds until he found a rhythm and blues station. He lowered the volume then pondered for a moment before he leaned back and turned his gaze on her. "Maybe we can go out sometime."

She widened her eyes "Like, on a date?" She hadn't seen an invitation coming.

"Yeah, a date. Maybe dinner and a movie?"

Before she answered, something crashed against the house. She lurched across the couch and into Carlos' arms. "What was that?" Her heart thundered in her chest.

He leaned away and smiled at her. "I'm not sure, but I'm thankful for it."

A flush crept up her neck, and she realized her boldness. She slunk back to her side of the sofa and dragged the afghan around her again. "I'm sorry. I frighten easily."

"No need to apologize. Storms can be pretty scary." He stood. "I'll have a look outside and see if I can tell what caused the noise."

The wind squealed around the open door, fluttered the drapes and blew leaves into the house. Carlos only did a quick check of the front yard, shaking his head as he closed the door. "Someone's chaise lounge has taken up residence on your lawn. People forget to stash their lawn furniture in times like this. Doesn't take much to pick up something that light and hurl it a few hundred feet."

Linda sat straighter. "I just thought of something. What about your sister? Isn't she going to be worried about you?"

"She knows I can take care of myself. Besides, she's at my parent's house this weekend.

Probably not even storming there. I called and let her know I took care of the house before I came down here."

"Thank goodness. I was afraid…"

"Of what?" His brow arched.

"Afraid you'd have to leave. I'm not sure I can handle being alone."

"You might be in more danger than you know."

Her breath hitched. "What do you mean? Do you think the storm has worsened?"

"I wasn't talking about the storm. I meant with me. I find you very attractive, Linda."

Her cheeks warmed again. She stared into her lap and swallowed. "You're not so bad on the eyes either. Plus, I like your personality. I really would like to have that date you asked about earlier…if we survive this storm."

Carlos bounced to the center of the sofa, turned up the radio and dialed to the weather station in time for commercial announcements. Before long, the regular program resumed.

"The storm has fallen below the hurricane rating system." A resonating voice filled the room.

"Earlier we experienced category one winds, but the velocity has greatly reduced. The current wind speed is 45 miles per hour with occasional gusts of fifty to fifty-five. Looks like we've escaped with just a tropical storm this time." Carlos switched back to slow jazz and leaned back. "So where were we?"

"I think we were talking about dates." She grinned.

"That we were." He smiled. "Since you like the beach, maybe we could have a picnic and then take in a movie."

"Oh, I'd love that. Only, let's pick a day when the waves are a little less angry and the sky a tad bluer."

He scooted closer and rested his arm on the sofa's back. "But there's one thing I always like to know about a woman before I actually date her."

"Really? And what would that be," she asked teasingly. "Haven't I already told you everything about me?"

"It's not really a fact—a question you answer. More like something you can demonstrate for me."

His body heat seeped through the afghan. She no longer needed her blanket, and kicked it off. Demonstrate? Did she really want to ask what he meant?

The candles flickered as the wicks grew shorter, and the log still crackled in the fireplace. The slow song on the radio stirred feelings she hadn't experienced in a long time, and the report about the storm put her more at ease.

Boldly inching over beneath his extended arm, she propped her feet on the coffee table. Her curiosity overcame the reservations screaming 'beware', and she turned her inquiring gaze on him. "So what exactly do I need to demonstrate?"

"You might say it's more of a test than a demonstration." His hand cupped her shoulder.

Apprehension stole her courage and she stared

straight ahead. "Okay, I give up." She cast a sidelong glance at him. "What kind of test are we talking about exactly?"

He cupped her chin and turned her face to him. Slowly, he leaned in, lowered his mouth to hers and claimed a kiss. Her breath halted for a moment, but she parted her lips, welcoming the soft intrusion of his tongue and the slight fluttering in her stomach. He tasted sweet and warm, and his body grazing her breasts unleashed butterflies in her belly. She caressed the side of his face, wanting more, needing more.

Without apparent reason, he pulled away, sat straight and stared into space. He massaged his chin with this thumb and forefinger, seeming deep in thought.

Confusion niggled at Linda, but she waited for an explanation. Finally she couldn't stand the silence any longer. "Want to explain?"

"Sure. What I like to know before I date someone is how they kiss. I was deciding how to rate the storm you just released in me. Remember, the weatherman said we'd escaped a category 'one' hurricane?"

"Yes, but I'm really not sure what he meant by that."

Carlos clasped his hands behind his head and smiled. "Well, the stronger the rating, the more damage predicted. In this case, I'm using emotion as a predictor. With one being the least and five, which is catastrophic in weather lingo, I'd have to give you a four and half."

"Four and a half? Is that good or bad?"

He pulled her across his body, her head resting in the crook of his arm. He peered into her eyes, the dying flames of the fire dancing in his. "That's good. Very, very good," he whispered in a low growl. "And I have no doubt that's not the best you can do."

Carlos lowered his head to claim her lips again. The

lights flickered and came back. Linda groaned. "Hold that thought." She rose, went to the switch and flicked off the lamp, then returned to the sofa, but sat next to him. "Better?"

He reeled her closer. "Much. The storm might have died down outside, but there's a lot of energy building in here."

She waggled a finger at him. "Yep, the temperature has notched up quite a bit, but you're going to have to wait at least until after our first date before you find out if I can improve my kiss rating."

He frowned, but nodded.

More than anything, she wanted to whisk him to her bedroom and sample what he most certainly would freely surrender, but inside her head, she couldn't ignore her morality, and the imaginary flashing neon, "Hurricane warning…love predicted."

The End

Hurricane Warning

The Forget-Me-Nots

The darkness seemed appropriate, but Sarah Palmer switched on the small lamp sitting atop the bedside table in her mother's bedroom. The familiar flowery scent of talcum hung in the air and plucked at Sarah's heart. For years, she'd watched Mom sprinkle powder between her sheets to give them a satiny feel and fresh smell. Although the talc created a hazy dust on the mahogany furniture, she never seemed to mind.

Voices from the living room indicated more people had arrived from the funeral. The mingled aromas of casseroles drifted down the hallway. Sarah still couldn't believe her mother was dead. Her empty rocker sat in the corner, looking desolate; her Bible lay on the table next to it. She always spent the hours before bedtime reading the "good book."

Sarah had often heard that recently deceased spirits adhered to those still living. She sat in the chair, leaned back and tried to feel Mom's presence, but the awful truth struck her. The woman who raised her was gone forever—at least from the mortal world.

"Sarah, are you here?" Her sister, Melinda, called from the hallway.

"In Mom's room."

Mel appeared in the doorway. Mom had always said despite their four-year age difference, her daughters were carbon copies of one another, with their blonde hair, blues eyes and slim builds.

"What are you doing all by yourself?" Mel asked. "Come on and join everyone else."

"If you don't mind, I'd rather stay in here. I'm not in the mood to put on a happy face and talk about the good old days. I miss her so much."

"So do I. She was my mother too, you know." Mel flashed a weak smile.

"I know, and I realize you feel her loss as much as I do, but I've never been away from home like you have. What am I going to do when I wake up tomorrow, and the day after, and she's not here?"

"You'll survive like we all will. Just because I have John and the kids doesn't lessen the pain, but time will. Remember how we thought the world ended when Daddy died. It didn't. Try to picture him and Mom together again, and happy. The image helps, believe me."

Melinda came and sat on the bed's edge and crooked one knee beside her. "I plan to stay a few extra days to help go through Mom's stuff. We have to decide what do with everything, like her clothes and shoes."

Sarah stood and walked to the ornate wooden box on the dresser. She turned, her hand on the top. "Would you mind if I went through Mom's jewelry and picked out a special keepsake?"

"Of course not. Take whatever you want. We're not going to be like some families who develop claws and fangs over a loved-one's personal belongings."

Melinda peered up at Sarah. "When did you get so tall? It seems like just yesterday you were ten and now you're twenty and in college. Where has time gone?"

Sarah shook her head. "I don't know. At times, I long to be a kid again, then Mom could still spoil me rotten.

I always liked being the baby of the family."

The doorbell rang. Mel stood, patted Sarah's arm and meandered out toward the living room. Sarah picked up the small mahogany chest that matched the other furniture pieces in the room and walked back to the rocking chair and sat. Tears stung the back of her eyes.

She fingered the scalloped edges around the top and the gold plate bearing the initials "CP." When she opened the box, her mother's favorite scent wafted out, stirring a wealth of memories. Sarah doubted she could ever smell lavender again and not think of Mom. The contents sparkled in the lamplight.

The first tier held nothing of sentimental value. The contents were mostly costume jewelry: earrings, necklaces and rings set with a myriad of faux gemstones. A few decorative holiday pins lay beneath. Sarah looked lovingly at the Santa Claus one her mother had worn last Christmas. Next to it, the ceramic daisy broach she and Melinda had given her years ago as a Mother's Day present. Some of the white painted leaves were chipped and cracked, and the yellow center had faded with age. There were too many emotions packed inside for Sarah to handle.

She set the jewelry box aside, moved over and stretched out on the bed. Her grief overwhelmed her when she smelled Mom's sheets. When all her tears were spent, she listened to muted voices in the other room until she drifted off to sleep.

****

"Sarah, wake up." Mel's voice invaded the silence. "Everyone has gone home. I thought you might want to go

107

up to your own room."

She sat and rubbed her eyes. "I think I'll sleep in here tonight."

Her sister nodded. She leaned against the doorjamb and crossed her arms. "You should've come in the living room and listened to all the stories people shared. Mom would have been so proud to hear the wonderful things said about her."

"Maybe she did hear..." Sarah shrugged. "But, I didn't need to listen to someone else's memories to remind me what a wonderful mother I have... or had." Sarah knuckled away a tear.

Melinda stretched. "Well, get some rest. Tomorrow will be brighter, I promise. This has been an emotional day for all of us." She walked over and planted a kiss on Sarah's cheek. "Goodnight, sis."

A loose step creaked under Melinda's weight, the guestroom door closed, and the house fell still. Mel's ability to remain stoic at such an emotional time annoyed Sarah. Perhaps her sister had used the months Mom battled cancer to prepare herself for this day. Maybe Mel just had more strength.

Sarah slid off the bed, picked up the jewelry box again and returned to the rocking chair. She removed the top tier, put it on the side table and ticked through the pieces on the bottom. Her gaze rested on three charm-like bars joined together with a black ribbon. She picked them up and dangled them in the air. Small flowers decorated the ends, and something had been etched on each. The metal discoloration made most of the writing illegible. Sarah squinted and barely made out part of a date: April, 1941. She couldn't see the actual day, but the month and year meant nothing to her. It wasn't a birthday, anniversary or holiday with which she was familiar.

Her interest in the other ornate pieces within the box paled once she found the charms. Where had they come from and what did they mean? Maybe Melinda knew something about them. She'd ask her first thing in the morning.

****

Melinda shrugged. "No, I've never seen them." She held the charms up for a closer peek. "They look very old."

"They are." Sarah reached across the breakfast table and snatched them back. "There's a month and date on one. April 1941; does that mean anything to you?"

Her sister laughed. "That's before my time. I wasn't born until 1952. Mom and Dad met in 1945 and married in '46, so I don't have a clue. Maybe they belong to someone else." She took a sip of coffee and went back to eating her muffin.

"How can you not wonder about them? Mom must have had them for a reason."

"I'm sure she did, but since we can't ask her, what makes them so important to you?" Melinda's brow furrowed.

"I'm not sure. Just call me curious." Sarah stuffed them into her pants pocket and picked at her own muffin. The blueberries were a little tangier than she expected.

"Mel stood and carried her empty cup to the sink. "Are you ready to get started going through Mom's closet?"

"Not really, but…"

"I know you'd prefer to wait, but since I'm here to help, we may as well get it over with."

Sarah took a deep breath. "You're right. I'm sure I wouldn't find it a pleasant task no matter how long I stalled." She followed Melinda to their mother's room.

Her heart ached as they cleaned the closet and boxed Mom's wardrobe for donation to the Salvation Army. Each piece of clothing elicited a memory of a loving parent now laid to rest in a cemetery across town—the dress she wore to Mel's wedding, the old shorts she donned to work in the garden. The thought of Mom being buried made Sarah shudder.

Melinda taped the top of the last box an hour later. "Well, that does it."

Sarah hefted it into her arms and nodded toward others. "If you help me carry these out to the car, I'll drive them over to the donation site and drop them off." She needed a rest from the tedious and painful task. Besides, it gave her an opportunity to stop by the jewelry store and ask a few questions about the charms.

****

Sarah fidgeted while the jeweler used a special polish to clean the tarnished surface of the first sterling bar. He finished and handed it to her. "Looks like this one says Clara."

"That was my mother's name." Sarah looked at the now-visible letters and nodded.

The glasses balanced on the man's nose made his pores look huge. Sarah wanted to push the frame up where it belonged, but instead gazed through the glass counter at wristwatches until he finished with the next charm.

"Here's number two."

She took the charm. The day was crystal clear, along with month and year. April 14, 1941. She closed her eyes and searched her memory for some association with the date. Mom had never mentioned anything about her life previous to Dad. Maybe the clue was on the final charm. Sarah chewed her bottom lip and waited.

"Number three. Do you know someone named Leon?" The man dangled the charm in the air.

Sarah shook her head and snared the third piece from him. "Never heard of anyone called that."

The jeweler stood with a blank expression, as if waiting for something. Sarah's cheeks warmed. She clasped the charms tight in one hand and reached for her wallet with the other. "I'm sorry. How much do I owe you?"

He held up a hand. "No charge. Can I do anything else for you today?"

"You've been very helpful already, but I wonder if you've ever seen anything like these before—know what they're called?" She opened her palm and spread the charms apart.

He smiled. "As a matter of fact I have." He took one and placed it on the counter. "I've seen them in my 'collectibles' book." Pulling a magnifying glass from a shelf behind him, he held it over the sterling piece. "See those little flowers on the end? They're called Forget-Me-Nots, and also the name given to this particular type of keepsake."

Sarah bent and viewed the small blossoms intricately placed on the bar's end, then glanced up. "What significance do they hold, if any?"

"The charms were very popular during World War II. They were given in friendship and collected until one had enough to create an entire bracelet. I don't know much more about them, but I'm sure you can research the Internet for more information."

"I will." Sarah's heart raced. She wasn't sure if it was from excitement or the anxiety of not knowing who Leon was. She couldn't wait to tell Melinda.

****

After relaying the jeweler's explanation about the charms, Sarah put the newly-polished bars on the table in front of her sister. "Now that all the tarnish is gone, you can clearly see what's engraved on each. One has Mom's name, another the April date, and the third says, Leon."

"Who the heck is Leon?"

Sarah sighed. "I was hoping you knew."

"Nope. Never heard of him." She picked one up and studied it. "They're kinda pretty though, now that they're shiny and new looking. What are you going to do with them? Are they worth anything because of their age?"

"I'm keeping them, of course. And I intend to find out the secret behind them." She held out her palm and wiggled her fingers until her sister returned the charm.

****

Without Melinda there, Sarah rattled around in the empty house. She'd taken a few extra days off from college to tie up more loose ends, but her thoughts never drifted far from the Forget-Me-Not charms. She'd even searched more thoroughly through her mother's room, hoping to find a journal or diary that made mention of this mysterious "Leon." There were no clues.

After going through paperwork in the desk, she

chanced upon a picture of her Aunt Lettie. It suddenly occurred to Sarah maybe the woman knew something. She was only a few years younger than Mom had been. Sarah hadn't visited her in quite a while, and had only exchanged a brief hug at the funeral, but this certainly provided a reason to drop by. Eager for answers, her fingers trembled as she dialed her aunt's number.

"Aunt Lettie, this is Sarah. I wonder if I could stop in for a visit—this afternoon perhaps."

"Sarah, dear. Of course. You're always welcome. Can you come around two o'clock? We'll have tea."

"Sure. I'll see you then." Sarah hung up, anxious to see how much her mother's sister was willing to share.

****

The china cup clinked against the matching saucer when Sarah placed the set on the rosewood coffee table. "Thank you, Auntie, I haven't had hot tea in quite a while. Mom always preferred coffee."

The older woman held her cup with an arched pinky finger. "Yes, your mother and I always had such different taste in everything, it seems. It's still so very hard for me to believe she's gone."

Sarah sighed. "I keep expecting to hear her in the kitchen or run into her in the hallway. The house is so empty without her."

Aunt Lettie, unlike her sister, had allowed her hair to go completely gray and had packed on some extra pounds over the years. She set her cup down and folded her hands in her lap. "I'm very glad she had everything in order when she passed. She was quite careful to make sure the house was paid for and in your name so you'd have a place to live. I know your sister will be mentioned quite generously in the will, too. Your mother shared her intentions with me and asked me to be the executor, and I agreed."

"Mom mentioned that to me. I'm very thankful to you."

"She would have done the same for me. We were quite close when we were younger. Marriage and children have a way of making people drift apart. We both were so wrapped up with our own families, you know."

"Yes, you've both been devoted mothers and wives. Tell me, Aunt Lettie, what was Mom like before she met Dad?"

"Whatever do you mean, dear?"

"Oh, I might as well just ask you…" Sarah reached in her purse and pulled out a plastic bag holding the charms. She took each one out and placed them gingerly on the coffee table.

Aunt Lettie leaned over, then glanced up and smiled. "For heaven sakes, where did you find those?"

"In Mom's jewelry box. Can you tell me about them?"

"Of course. I remember as if the first time I saw them was yesterday." Her aunt stood and went to the bookcase across the room. She returned with a photo album and sat on the couch, alongside Sarah.

The pictures inside were reminiscent of old war movies; the hairstyles, the floral dresses, the pillbox hats and thick-heeled shoes. Sarah's eyes widened at a much younger version of her mother and Aunt Lettie, wearing aprons and standing behind a serving table. She glanced to her aunt. "Where were these photos taken?"

"Your mother and I worked the USO dances during the war. Didn't she ever tell you?"

"No, this is the first I've heard about it. Besides stories of childhood, her life seemed to begin when she met Daddy. I see now she left out a chapter." Sarah smiled. "Please go on."

Aunt Lettie turned a page and pointed to a snapshot of Sarah's mom dishing up a piece of pie for a young soldier. "This G.I. took a shine to your mother. He came every week just to see her and wouldn't accept food from anyone else."

"Did Mom like him, too?"

The woman shook her head. "No, the attraction was purely one-sided. Clara never acted like they were more than friends, but you could see in his eyes he wanted more."

Sarah reached over and picked up a charm. "His name wouldn't happen to be Leon, would it?"

"It would. I remember the day Leon brought those charms to your mother."

"So, she got these from a soldier."

"Yes." Aunt Lettie set the album aside and picked up one of the remaining bars. "It was the exact day etched here—April 14, 1941. He handed her a tiny box tied with a red ribbon. Your mother was reluctant to accept his gift, and tried to refuse, but Leon insisted. He told her he was getting shipped out the next day—going to one of the most active fronts at the time. Said the contents were just something to remember him by in case he didn't make it back."

"Did he? Make it back, I mean." Sarah nodded, hoping.

"I'm not sure. We never saw him again. He kissed your mother on the cheek and left before she opened the box."

"And you're positive she never laid eyes on him again?" Sarah's mouth gaped.

"No. We often wondered what happened to him. So many young men lost their lives. We both prayed for him that night. Your mother cried when she read the note he'd put inside the box. I cried when she shared it with me."

"Do you remember what it said?"

"Like I just read it yesterday." She lapsed into a nostalgic moment, a smile on her face and her eyes fixed on nothingness. Her mind seemingly churned out memories.

I've gone to war to pay my due
I leave behind these charms with you.
If for some reason I don't come back.
Tie these together with a ribbon of black...and Forget-Me-Not."

Tears gathered in Sarah's eyes. Had the young man survived the war? Had he gone on to marry another and spend a happy life as her mother had? The answers would forever remain a mystery, but more importantly, he'd never know the trinkets he left behind provided much more than sweet memories. They gave a grieving daughter a welcome glimpse of her mother's youth and a special commemoration to one day pass on to her own children. Until she'd found the charms, she hadn't known much about Forget-Me-Nots, but suddenly they'd become her favorite flower.

The End

Paging Dr. Jones

"Code blue, code blue!"

Catherine McGuire heard the paging system calling out the strange announcement. She'd seen the term used on TV programs often enough to know someone was in terrible trouble. Was she the one?

The sensation of intense pain gripped her as she wracked her foggy brain, trying to remember what'd happened. She recalled starting to back the car out of the driveway, but nothing beyond that.

Like a fog rising from a shrouded lake, her mind cleared. She'd had another terrible argument with her ex-husband, Stan. His angry words echoed in her mind. *I'll make sure no man will ever look at you.*

The clarity of the vision in her head caused her to gasp—him dragging her from the car, the rage that narrowed his eyes and pulled his full lips into a feral grin. Oh, what had he done this time?

The speed with which her gurney moved down the hospital corridor blurred the holes in the acoustical ceiling tiles and made her dizzy. The rapid pace of the medical team caused scuffling echoes in the silence.

Unable to turn her head away from the muted-colored walls, she vaguely noticed someone holding an IV bag. Was the infusing liquid traveling down the tube going to save her? Only God knew. Catherine prayed for salvation. She had lots of life to live, being only thirty and starting anew. Death frightened her and hovered way too close at the moment. She teetered on the edge of a dark abyss.

The movement ceased, and the prodding and poking began. Her clothing, quickly stripped away, left her body exposed and prickled with goose bumps. Was it unshed tears that clouded her vision? She couldn't tell. The chattering of her teeth refused to stop no matter how hard she tried. Finally, someone covered her with a warmed blanket and the chill passed, but now her temples pounded in painful rhythm to the fearful beat of her heart. Fear increased the cadence.

A chorus of shouted directions in the exam room eventually melded into one loud voice, but none of what was said made sense. Her eyelashes fluttered as she fought to remain awake, but the din grew muffled as darkness beckoned to her.

"Quick, get the code cart!" Those dreadful words were the last she heard before she surrendered to escape from the pain and pandemonium.

****

"Mrs. McGuire?" A deep, yet soft, resonating voice called out to her. "Can you hear me? If you can, please squeeze my finger."

Catherine mustered her strength and squeezed while a myriad of questions flooded her mind. Even her throat hurt. "I-I hear you, but where am I. What happened to me?" Her voice was reduced to a whisper.

She struggled to open her eyes only to find she couldn't see. Something covered her face, and when she raised a hand to investigate, a piecing pain stabbed at her side. A warm hand enveloped hers and lowered it to the bed.

"Now, now, don't touch." The voice was strange, but friendly. "I'm Dr. Jones, your attending physician. You're…you're badly injured and in the hospital. I'm afraid you were severely beaten, and your face took the brunt of the punishment. You won't be able to see for a while because we've bandaged your eyes, and it's best you don't disturb the dressing."

She shifted her position ever so slightly and moaned.

"You're going to experience pain, so we've connected you to a morphine pump. Whenever you need an infusion, all you need do is press the button to send medication directly into your IV."

He placed the control in her hand.

Again, her words came in an inaudible whisper. "Thank you."

Dr. Jones patted her arm. "Your larynx was also injured, so speaking is going to be difficult for a time. I'd prefer if you limit your attempts to give your body time to heal."

"Eyes?" She disobeyed his orders and squeaked out one word because she needed to know. The possibility of being blind scared her to death. Her muscles tensed while awaiting his answer.

"Your eyes are quite swollen from the beating you received, and I'm concerned about possible vision loss. I've put in some medicated drops, and plan to have an ophthalmologist check your eyes thoroughly. Please try not to worry."

Right, like that was easy, especially when she had a million questions she couldn't ask. Hell, she didn't even know what day it was.

Frustration welled inside her like a growing child then subsided as a haze of drowsiness claimed her. She dozed off.

****

Dr. Jones' conversation with Catherine's roommate, Cassandra, left him pondering. Even a year after her divorce, Catherine's ex-husband still harassed her when he drank. During their five-year marriage, he'd beaten her on a regular basis, but his causing her to miscarry had been the final straw. Catherine moved in with her friend, and filed for a divorce and a restraining order.

Obviously the order of protection didn't do much good. He shook his head, slowly.

Standing outside the cubicle where she slept, he rubbed his furrowed brow, and studied her sleeping form. What in the world would drive a man to beat a woman so badly? Catherine's face would be unrecognizable to anyone who knew her, so bruised and swollen. Probably her ex learned the trait from his dad…most wife-beaters did.

Looking so frail, with her eyes swathed in bandages and her small stature dwarfed by the hospital bed, she whimpered, even in slumber. He perused her features trying to imagine what she looked like before the beating, but he couldn't conjure what lay beneath the inflicted damage.

The thin blanket covering her molded perfectly to the outline of her body and revealed a slim figure---firm, jutting breasts and curves in all the right places. He sighed and with a deep breath, chased away his improper thoughts. Good God, the woman was an assault victim and he was admiring her body. He needed to get a grip on his emotions.

From pity to promiscuous in such a short time showed how ridiculous his thoughts.

The day had been a long one. He ran a hand thought his hair and yawned. He was on a sixteen-hour rotation as the ER doctor on call, but was catching a nap in between seeing patients when Catherine arrived. He thought he'd seen it all, but he'd never get used to senseless beatings.

He worked with one of the best trauma teams in the state, so she'd received excellent care. The preliminary examination revealed hairline fractures of her cheekbone, nose, and two ribs, and what didn't require surgery would heal on its own. Unfortunately, her recovery would be painful and slow. His greatest worry was her vision. Any damage to the optic nerve, retina or cornea would easily impair her sight, and that wasn't his domain—he was a general medicine doctor.

Besides the looming threat of vision loss, she might need reconstructive surgery. That decision wouldn't be made until the swelling subsided. Despite what people thought about money-hungry doctors, he prayed she didn't need to face anything else. She'd been through enough pain already.

With curled fists, he rubbed the tiredness from his eyes and turned to leave, but Catherine stirred. "Is someone there?" Her question came out in a choked whisper, but still audible.

He brushed past the curtain and walked closer to her bed. "Yes, Ms. McGuire. It's me, Dr. Jones, remember?"

"Am I going to die?" Her voice trembled.

Unprepared for that question, he curled his fingers into a fist, sending his nails biting into his palm. Damn her ex for putting him in this position. "Ah…of course not.

You're going to be fine. You might need a few minor surgical procedures, but we have to wait and see how your healing progresses. By my estimate, you'll make a complete recovery."

He hoped what he told her wasn't a lie.

He patted her hand. "Now, you need to rest your voice, and trust me and the hospital staff. I have another patient to look in on before my shift ends, but I'll be back in the morning. By then, you'll most likely have been moved to a regular room so someone can keep a closer eye on you. You're in good hands here."

****

Catherine awoke to pain. The surrounding darkness frightened her for a split second, but then she remembered her face was in bandages. Sporadic memories dotted her mind, among them, the doctor's description of her injuries.

She hesitated to move, recalling the searing pain resulting from just raising her arm, but her head throbbed, and she needed pain medicine.

Recalling, the morphine pump, she blindly searched the sheets for the control she'd dropped during sleep. Her fingertips grazed the smooth flesh of another hand.

"Are you looking for this?" The same voice she recalled sliced the silence. He pressed the control button in her palm.

"Thanks." She risked a whisper and quickly released the drug into her IV. Wooziness engulfed her, but she breathed a sigh of relief. Was it morning? Had she slept through the night? At least her throat felt better.

"I didn't expect to find you still in the ER." His

voice resonated with a much more rested tone. "I guess they couldn't find an empty bed for you. Hope you slept well. These gurneys aren't the most comfortable."

"So, it is morning?" She rasped.

"It is, and I'm checking your chart and it looks like you slept well all night. The ophthalmologist will be here tomorrow so we should learn something more about your eyes." Metal clinked as he spoke. She imagined a file making contact with the securing rail.

He touched her hand from the opposite side of the gurney. "In ten words or less, tell me how you're feeling."

Darn…why didn't he stay in one place? She'd turned her head toward where she expected him to be and now she had to move again. "I can actually talk without much pain today."

"That's good, but don't overdo it." His soft fingers touched her cheek. "Once this swelling goes down, we'll see what we're really dealing with and plan from there."

Swelling? Her mind traveled backwards. "Stan, did this to me. Again. Why can't he just go away and leave me alone?" The hair on the back of her neck bristled. Would her life always be like this? The bandages hid the tears but her body convulsed in sobs.

"Mrs. McGuire…are you okay?"

"Yes…I'm fine." She lied and endured a painful breath to compose.

"When you're ready, we can talk about what happened, but it might help if you spoke to an actual counselor."

"I-I don't want to talk to one. What happened is too embarrassing."

"There's no need to feel that way. You didn't do

anything wrong."

"Except be stupid and stay with someone who continued to beat me…and never make him pay…."

"How does your throat feel when you speak?"

"A little raspy, but barely any pain at all."

Something scraped against the floor.

"Then, how about talking to me?" His voice indicated he'd sat. "Counseling isn't my forte, but I know for a fact if you unburden yourself, you'll feel better. Is there anyone we can contact for you…parents, friends?"

She tensed and attempted to sit up. "No!" Her elevated tone didn't quite result in a scream."

The chair legs squealed and his voice came from above her. He urged her back onto her pillow. "Whoa, careful there. I didn't mean to upset you."

She trembled beneath his hands. "Sorry. I don't want anyone to know I'm here. I haven't had contact with my parents for years…and I'm sure they'll be more than happy to say, 'I told you so.'"

Pity welled in his heart. How awful to not have contact with the people who brought you into the world, and even worse, fear their judgment.

"You are aware we had to contact the police?" He hated telling her and waited for another outburst.

"Police? Oh my God, why?"

"It's standard procedure whenever there's an assault involved. Surely, you don't want your ex to get away with this?"

"Reporting him will only make him madder." She lowered her head and massaged the back of her neck. "I've been through this already. I call, they arrest him, he makes bail, drinks to ease his anger, gets even more irate and comes looking for me to be his punching bag. I can't take it anymore." Sobs consumed her again.

He clenched his teeth at upsetting her and smoothed her disheveled blonde hair. "There has to be a way for the law to protect you. If there is a next time, he could kill you."

She relaxed beneath his touch, still hiccupping from unseen tears. "That's exactly what he wants to do. No one can protect me. He's already said if he can't have me, no one will."

"You're wrong. You can take charge, but you have to start the process here and now. Follow through with your complaint against him. By allowing him to get away with bad behavior time and time again, you're telling him you approve of his actions. Show him you're not! I imagine it's not easy, but take a stand now or prepare to spend the rest of your life like this."

Counseling wasn't his forte, but she needed to hear what he said. Had he gone too far? Regardless, he meant every word. "I hope you'll think about what I've said." He turned to leave.

Catherine grasped blindly at his sleeve. "No, please don't go. I'm afraid."

For some reason beyond his comprehension, he couldn't refuse. Even though a virtual stranger, he heard her beauty in her voice…even beneath the bruises and swelling. He plucked her clutching fingers from his arm then placed her arm back beneath her blanket. He fluffed her pillows and pondered her request.

"Well…I've finished my rounds, so I suppose I can stay for a while. You're really quite safe here, so…" He reached into his lab coat and brought out a small book. "Do you like poetry?" He sat.

"I love it. Are you going to recite some?" The little chuckle in her voice was a nice change.

"No, I carry some of my favorites with me. Reading is my way to relax when things get hectic. Some people do yoga, I do poems…sonnets actually."

He opened the book and started to read.

She swells within my dreams,
there always within my reach, but not.
Her memory haunts my nights,
for she is the pattern after which forms true love.
I despise the darkness, for on moonless nights,
my dreams betray my heart.
I sense her face and reach to touch her silk skin.
She is not there,
and I wake and cry.
cry for love lost and not found again in this lifetime.
Cruel is the night.

That's beauti—." She yawned, and drowsiness edged her words. "Who wrote…? She winced when she tried to cover her mouth.

"How about you take a nap and I come back and read some more later?" He closed the book.

"It's a deal. I'm suddenly very sleepy, and I don't want to miss a line."

He stood and watched as she snuggled beneath the covers. She had no idea he was there, and how much he longed to soothe the brow beneath her bandage. Why had he read his personal thoughts to her? His fingers ruffled the pages he'd placed back in his pocket.

His habit of jotting down his feelings had produced his own sonnet collection. He loved to write, and during a psych class in college, the teacher had mentioned the healing properties of keeping a journal. Sometimes, his written words soothed his soul.

Doctor's suffered from incredible loneliness at times. Medical school, interning…duty took all their time and left none for personal relationships. He hadn't been serious with anyone since his high school sweetheart, and losing her had been the impetus behind the verses he wrote. Oh, he'd dated, but hadn't found his soul mate again. Where had life taken his Angela, his first and only true love? Hopefully to places happier than Catherine McGuire.

****

Catherine awoke to strange beeps in the distance. Something about her surroundings were different. She blindly felt for the familiar gurney rails, and immediately recognized she'd been moved to a real bed. That morphine had really knocked her out. Maybe she'd used it too freely. In her grappling, her searching fingers found buttons. She pushed one. A voice blared from toward the ceiling. She pushed another until the noise lowered. A third push elevated the head of her bed…a fourth, the foot. She manipulated those buttons until she found a comfortable position.

"You rang?" A feminine voice sounded next to her.

"I'm sorry. I really don't need anything, I was just pushing buttons to find out what happens when I do."

"That's okay, Mrs. McGuire. You obviously found the one you need to summon help, so I don't need to show you how to use the controls." The woman chuckled.

"When did I get here?" Catherine asked.

"They brought you up last night. We had an opening and Dr. Jones requested you be transferred out of the ER."

A lump formed in Catherine's throat. "So, I won't be seeing him anymore?"

"Oh, I'm sure you will. He said to tell you he'd stop by as soon as he found time. Now, I have to get back to the desk. Would you like to listen to the TV?"

"No, I'm fine. Maybe I'll just take a nap. I can't seem to get past this drowsiness."

"I'm sure the medication they've had you on contributes to the problem. We've taken you off the morphine and if you need something for the pain, just let me know and I'll add something to your IV that isn't quite so strong."

"Thank you."

Footsteps clicked against the floor. "Oh, and Dr. Jones said something about poetry tonight." The nurses' voice came from further across the room. "I'm not sure what that means."

"Oh, I do." Catherine warmed at more reading of such warming thoughts. She couldn't forget to ask who wrote them. Snuggling down, she pulled the sheet up to chin with her unencumbered hand, and found a comfortable position for the one pierced by the IV needle. She heaved a contented sigh and drifted off to strains of violin music in her mind.

****

Hospitalized for five days and still unable to see, Catherine released a loud breath, reflecting her boredom. Even sightless, she'd run a brush through her long hair and sat up much straighter in bed than she previously had. Dr. Jones' visits had made the evenings much more tolerable, and she looked forward to tonight and more of his poetic readings. How she wished she could watch the minutes tick by on a clock.

After what seemed an eternity, she heard footsteps in her room. "Hello."

"It's me, Catherine." Dr. Jones' voice resonated in the soundless room.

"Oh, it must be evening. I have no idea of the time or even the day. Do you have any idea how long I have to contend with these blasted bandages?"

"Didn't the eye doctor tell you he wants you to wear them a while longer…at least until the swelling around your eyes has completely abated?"

"I vaguely remember his visit, what with so many people checking out various parts of me."

"Have the police been to see you yet?"

"Yes. They arrested Stan, and this time, they assured me because of his past record, he'll serve a lengthy sentence. No bail for him this time."

"That should make you feel better."

She smiled. "You have no idea. Marrying him was the biggest mistake of my life. I just didn't know it at the time. It wasn't long after our wedding that I realized he wasn't the one for me…just someone to fill a void. I never got over loving my first boyfriend, and I guess I'm destined to have feelings for him for the rest of my life."

"Trust me, I understand. What caused you two to break up?"

"My father got a new job and moved the family to another state. Of course, both he and my mother downplayed my feelings, attributing my heartbreak to puppy love. They forbade me to have any contact with him and threatened to take away all my privileges if I disobeyed. I'd just learned to drive, and the thought of giving up my license was what made me agree."

"Do you wish you'd ignored their threats?"

"Oh, of course. Then I might have been happily married, with children instead of having walked down the aisle with Stan." She curled her lip in disdain.

"At least you won't have to worry about him brutalizing you again."

"And I'm so relieved. Stan was a drinker, and a mean one. It took me five years to get up the courage to leave him, and finally, because you gave me the strength to take a stand, I don't have to play the role of a scared little mouse anymore."

Her thoughts turned to Wes, her high school love, and she pondered what life might have been like married to him. The football quarterback, he'd been everyone girl's dream—handsome, dark hair, chocolate eyes, and a killer smile.

She recalled the tummy butterflies he released with his first kiss. She ran her fingertips across her lips, trying to recapture the moment. Sadly, she pushed the thoughts aside. He probably had long ago forgotten her.

Catherine turned her attention to where she imagined the good doctor stood. "Are you going to read for me tonight?"

"I'm afraid not." His voice came from a distance. "I've been paged back to the ER, but I will check in with you again soon…if that's okay."

"Are you kidding? I'd probably go stark-raving mad

without your visits. I'll try to resist jogging the hallways until you return." She laughed and waved. "See you…or rather *hear* you."

****

Catherine awoke, supposing a new day shined outside her window. She raised herself into a sitting position, searched for her brush and drew long strokes through hair she imagined was snarled and in disarray.

"Good morning, Mrs. McGuire…it's time for your vitals."

Catherine put away her brush and offered her arm. The nurse stuck a thermometer in Catherine's mouth then carefully wrapped the blood pressure cuff around her upper arm. "Tell me if I hurt you." She removed the thermometer at the beep and proceeded to pump measuring air into the armband.

"Surprisingly, I don't feel nearly as sore today."

The sound of air whooshed as the cuff released.

"Your face is looking much better." The nurse grasped Catherine's wrist with two fingers and her thumb. "I see yellow hues replacing the angry purple that's been there for days."

"That's good. Purple has never been my favorite color."

"You still have a ways to go before you're completely healed, but this is a good start. Dr. Corday will be in today to check your eyes again. Can I get you anything before I go?"

"No, I suppose breakfast will be here anytime. I just need my coffee."

"I passed the cafeteria staff on my way in to your room. They should be getting here any minute. I'll be back later to give you a sponge bath and change your sheets."

Her footfall sounded as she left the room, but her voice returned. "Oh, Dr. Jones has a surgery consult scheduled for you and he wants to know if you have a current photo for comparison. Do you have one?"

Catherine thought a minute. She still had the proof from the picture on her telephone company ID badge. All employees had to wear one, even operators. "Yes, as a matter of fact, I do. My new job required I have one taken. I'll have my roommate bring it in."

"That'll work."

"Wait! Catherine summoned the nurse back. "Doctor Jones will be coming by tonight, right?"

"Darn! I forgot all about that. He's off tonight and tomorrow, but he'll see you when he's back on duty."

Catherine's mood faded to match the darkness surrounding her. After another reading, she'd learned he was the author, and there was something very special about him. Comfortable and kind, he was the kind of doctor she'd never met before, and his company had been instrumental to her healing. Obviously he felt some attraction or he wouldn't keep visiting. Assuming the nurse had left, Catherine lowered her bed and prayed for sleep to claim her from the boredom and disappointment.

****

Catherine was going stir crazy and tired of not being able to see. Listening to TV wasn't the same. She switched the set off, punched her pillow, and rolled to her side.

"Hi, how are you feeling?" The voice brought light to her darkness and raised her spirits.

She turned over on her back and raised the head of her bed some. "I'm fine, thanks. According to Dr. Corday, I get this dumb bandage off tomorrow and I'm drying to see if you look like you sound."

"And how do I sound?"

Like a handsome hunk. No, she didn't dare admit that, but she did enjoy the images in her mind. "I'd say tall, blond and muscular."

"Wrong on all counts." He laughed. "Well, even if you'll most likely be disappointed, at least I'll get to see how you look when you aren't black and blue."

"You won't even have to wait until tomorrow, and that's not fair." She pulled her lips into a pout.

"How so?"

"You asked for a picture of me and my roommate is bringing one in tonight. I'm sure you'll agree that while I'm no beauty queen, I look a hundred times better without the swelling and my gauze headband."

"I'm sure you're not making the fashion statement you'd hoped for, but I won't be needing the picture after all."

"Why not?"

"The specialist rechecked the x-ray of your cheek after he saw you this week, and as it turns out, all you need is a little aligning so the bone can heal properly. The fix requires just a minor procedure and one that won't leave any scarring. He has you scheduled for tomorrow so you can get out of this place. I'm sure you're more than ready."

Her fingertips grazed her cheek. "Like one more scar will matter. I shudder to think what I'm going to look like when all this goes away."

"You might be surprised." He patted her arm in a reassuring way. "The body is a wondrous thing—it heals wounds we never expect it would. I'd think you'd be jumping with joy at the thought of going home."

Strange, but his mention of leaving stirred reactions she didn't expect. She drew in a breath and struggled against the sadness creeping over her. Did she dare mention how much she'd miss him, or even state her desire to see him again? No...her brain screamed he was probably married.

His warm breath caressed her face; she suspected he was leaning closer. "Don't tell anyone, but you have a new friend who has excellent connections to great surgeons, so just in case...." The soft, secretive tone of his voice fluttered her heart.

Outside her room, he pondered the feelings she stirred in him. He barely knew her, but she possessed something oddly familiar and comfortable—something he couldn't quite figure out. Drawing from his sci-fi interest and watching paranormal movies, he considered they might have known one another in a different time and place. He rolled his eyes at such a far-fetched idea.

Taking his stethoscope from around his neck, he tucked it into the pocket of his lab coat. As he walked away from her room, a stanza from one of his first sonnets formed in his mind—the one he wrote for a high school English assignment and dedicated to his sweet Angela. *With grace and beauty, she walks the earth and warms my very soul.*

How strange. He hadn't thought of that verse in years. Maybe he'd write one for Catherine and present it to her before she went home.

****

Dressed in surgical scrubs, Dr. Jones stood at the nurses' station and checked Catherine's chart. "Is Mrs. McGuire ready for discharge."

"She will be momentarily. Dr. Corday is in removing her bandages right now," a nurse responded. The one seated at the counter stuck out her hand. "Oh, by the way…her friend asked me to give you her picture."

He shook his head. "I don't…." He changed his mind and took the glossy image offered him.

Leaning on the counter, he peered at the photograph. Catherine was beautiful, just as he'd imagined. Blonde hair, beautiful blue eyes, pearly white smile…something tugged at his heart.

"This is just too bizarre," he muttered as he studied the picture more closely. It couldn't be….

His heart pounded hard within his chest as he hurried into her room. Catherine stood with her back to him, looking out the window…her first time out of bed since the attack. Her hair cascaded well past her shoulders, and the reflecting sunlight cast a halo-like outline around her. Even in a drab hospital gown, her feminine shape was readily apparent.

He swallowed hard. "Mrs. McGu…Catherine?"

She turned. "Yes…" Feeling the blood drain from her face and her knees turn weak, she grasped the windowsill to steady herself.

Her mouth, dry as summer in the Sahara, shielded the words she tried to speak. "Oh…my God…is it really you? Wes…Wesley Jones? Is that you?"

"Yes." His brow arched. "But…but, I don't understand."

Steady on her feet now, she closed the gap between them. She caressed his cheek, her other hand on his chest. "I can't believe it's really you. Don't you remember who I am?"

"Angela?" His eyes widened.

"Yes, it's me."

"But…?"

"I know, I know. Catherine is my middle name and McGuire is Stan's last name. I haven't had a chance to change back to Ryan. Angela was the person who loved Wesley Jones, so I created a new me. I dropped the Angela, but I never forgot you."

Happy tears trickled down her cheeks. "Oh, Wes, I can't believe I've found you again." She so desired to draw him close and recapture all those lost years. But, what if he *was* married—belonged to someone else. Was this just another cruel trick of fate? Her mind spun. What if he no longer had feelings for her? Did he have a wife and kids? Her stomach churned with dread, waiting for him to speak.

Wes brushed a lock of hair from her forehead. "I'm speechless. So many years have passed since…"

"Did you marry?" The words bubbled out before she had a chance to stop them.

He splayed his fingers through his hair. "No, however, I see you—"

"Please don't judge marriage by the mistakes I've made. I should have walked away so many times, but…." She bit her knuckles and stared at the floor.

Wes cupped her chin and forced her to look at him. "I could never think badly of you."

"How could you not? I've been a fool for so long. I tried to believe Stan would change…wanted to—"

"Shhh." Wes touched his fingers to her lips. "There's no need to explain."

Her lips warmed beneath his touch. His piercing gaze told her he still had feelings, but she needed to hear him say the words…wanted to hear them. She grasped his hand and held it between both of hers. "So, tell me why you never married."

He smiled and shook his head. "Four years of college then medical school, interning, practicing. I've gone on lots of dates had plenty of opportunity to build relationships, but the truth is, I never found anyone to take your place. I love you so much…still do, as silly as that might sound."

Tears burned the back of her eyes. She shook her head. "There's nothing silly about your reasoning…in fact, I understand. I love you, too. Doesn't it feel like we've taken a big step back in time? Finding you has been my dream for years…a dream where we pick up like nothing happened to separate us. But…." She held him at arms length and glanced away. "This isn't how I imagined I'd appear. I must look awful." She turned her face. "Oh God, how can you even stand to see me like this?"

He snared her back into an embrace, forcing her gaze to his. "You're beautiful, and don't you forget it…not just on the outside, but the inside, too. I'm dying to kiss you, but I'm afraid I'll hurt you."

"I'll take the risk…just get the morphine back." She quipped with him but would gladly endure any pain for a taste of him.

He leaned in and brushed his lips against hers then

drew back and peered deeply into her eyes. "I couldn't imagine why I felt so at ease reading my sonnets to you…now I know why. I wrote them about you, so who better to hear them? I even recalled the very first one I ever wrote to you…you know the one when we were in high school. I can't believe I actually remembered it."

"You mean this one?" She took a step back and clasped hands with him. "With grace and beauty she walks the earth and warms my very soul…."

A smile spread across his face. "Yes, that's the one…'to hold her near through eternity shall be my heart's true goal.'" He completed the verse and gathered her into his arms.

"Calling Dr. Jones, calling Dr. Jones, report to the nurses' station, STAT!" The paging system interrupted their heartwarming moment.

"Oh no," he moaned, but held her tight. "Angela, I have to go, but I'll be back and then I'm never going to let you go again." His words ran together in a rush. "And when I return, I'm taking you home with me…forever." He turned and sped out the door.

Catherine stood in the middle of the room, her knees weak, but not for medical reasons this time. The warmth of Wes' kiss still lingered on her lips. She clasped a hand to her abdomen and gasped. After all these years, he still gave her tummy butterflies.

Her heart soared. How could life take such a wonderful turn? Something horrible had turned into a blessing, and she wasn't about to question her good fortune. She crawled back into bed, smiling and bidding farewell to all the bad memories and welcoming new ones yet to be made. She wasn't good at sonnets, but if her heart could write a news story, it would read: Angela Ryan resurfaced today after a long, painful absence and reunited with Dr. Wesley Jones, her high school and forever love.

The End…or perhaps just the beginning.

Paging Dr. Jones

About the Author

Born and raised in California, Ginger and husband Kelly, who happens to be her greatest fan, moved to Tennessee in 2004. Overcoming culture shock took a while, but she continues to write, finding inspiration in the vast number of southern historical areas. She's multi-published in several genres, but her favorite remains historical romance with a western flavor. Besides writing and promoting her work, she always manages to find time to enjoy her grandson, Spencer. The cheerful and patient way he deals with his autistic challenges inspires her to keep doing what she loves—being an author and his Nee Nee!

Other Books We Love Books By Ginger Simpson

Ages of Love
Destiny's Bride
First Degree Innocence
Sarah's Passion
Sarah's Heart
Ellie's Legacy
Time Invested
Culture Shock
Embezzled Love
A Novel Murder
Hattie's Heroes
Ginger Simpson Special Edition

Books We Love

http://bookswelove.net
and Books We Love Spice
http://spicewelove.com

Top quality books loved by readers,
Romance, Mystery, Fantasy, Suspense
Vampires, Werewolves, Cops, Lovers.
Young Adult, Historical, Paranormal